"Who are my name

"Doesn't matter.

He was taller than her, but no more than six feet or so in boots. Worn jeans were topped by a black T-shirt. He had good hands, she noted, and surprisingly long hair. Far too long for your average cop.

"It does to me. Look, I appreciate you saving my life, but I'm fine, now, and I really don't have time to play games."

He drew her closer until his mouth moved against her temple. "You need to go back to New York. No questions, no detours, just get on the highway and drive."

He used the fingers of his other hand to capture her chin. "Do it, Isabella. Now. While you can." Then he drew her closer still, set his mouth next to her ear and added a soft, "If you want to live, you need to get as far away from this house as possible."

JENNA RYAN

DARKWOOD MANOR

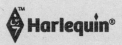

TORONTO NEW YORK LONDON
AMSTERDAM PARIS SYDNEY HAMBURG
STOCKHOLM ATHENS TOKYO MILAN MADRID
PRAGUE WARSAW BUDAPEST AUCKLAND

In Memory of Sheena

You were a strong, brave girl all through your life.
Now Heaven has a beautiful new angel.
Fly fast and free, sweet Little Pea.
We'll always be with you.
We'll always love you…

Recycling programs
for this product may
not exist in your area.

ISBN-13: 978-0-373-69526-3

DARKWOOD MANOR

Copyright © 2011 by Jacqueline Goff

www.eHarlequin.com

Printed in U.S.A.

ABOUT THE AUTHOR

Jenna started making up stories before she could read or write. Growing up, romance always had a strong appeal, but romantic suspense was the perfect fit. She tried out a number of different careers, including modeling, interior design and travel, but writing has always been her one true love. That and her longtime partner, Rod.

Inspired from book to book by her sister Kathy, she lives in a rural setting fifteen minutes from the city of Victoria, British Columbia. It's taken a lot of years, but she's finally slowed the frantic pace and adopted a West Coast mindset. Stay active, stay healthy, keep it simple. Enjoy the ride, enjoy the read. All of that works for her, but what she continues to enjoy most is writing stories she loves. She also loves reader feedback. Email her at jacquigoff@shaw.ca or visit Jenna Ryan on Facebook.

Books by Jenna Ryan

HARLEQUIN INTRIGUE

CAST OF CHARACTERS

Isabella Ross—Her ex-boyfriend left her a haunted mansion in Maine.

Donovan Black—He is a descendant of Darkwood Manor's malevolent original owner.

Katie Lynn Ross—Isabella's cousin disappears from the manor soon after their arrival.

Darlene Calvert—Donovan's cousin is desperate to get out of town.

George Calvert—Donovan's aunt feels like a prisoner of her own father's will.

Orry Lucas—The acting Sheriff has aspirations and more than a few secrets.

Gordie Tallahassee—The local Realtor sees a gold mine in the shadowy manor.

Robert Drake—The developer is hungry to purchase Darkwood Manor.

Prologue

The road that wound northward along the rocky Maine coast felt slick beneath the tires of David Morris Gimbel's vintage Corvette.

He grinned as the car jumped forward. You couldn't do speeds like this in the city, and a vehicle needed to stretch its legs every now and then. Plus the text message he'd received that afternoon had sounded urgent. He was considering the implications when his cell phone interrupted.

He glanced at the screen. "I'm twenty miles away, Haden. More problems?"

"Lights winking off and on," the man on the other end responded. "I've been hearing moans and thumps, too. Then, not five minutes ago, a wail that made every hair on my body stand up. Saw a shadow on the cliff, but it disappeared when the wail started."

David navigated a hard corner one-handed, squinted into the misty night. "Shadows are made by people. So are noises and light switches. Wail could've been a dog hunting for a mate."

"I've had three dogs in my time, Gimbel. None of 'em ever made a sound like that."

"Nineteen miles." David scoped the road before him. Unless his mental GPS had been thrown off by the moonless September night, he was two wide turns away from

Cemetery Point. He gunned it through number one and strove for patience.

"Lock your doors, draw your shades and pour a couple fingers of whiskey. The next sound you hear will be me screeching to a halt in front of your cottage."

"I can hear you screeching from here," the man retorted. "Aw, hell, I should've called my nephew instead of a non-believer like you."

The tires slipped, but David didn't back off the gas. "Since when do federal sharpshooters buy into the woo-woo scene? Pour the whiskey, Haden, and wait for my head—"

He broke off, swore sharply.

He heard Haden's gruff "Gimbel? You there?" right before his cell phone landed on the floor.

The silhouette of the guardrail was a blur, but he figured the nose of his car hit it at more than three times the posted limit. If ghosts existed, he was about to find out.

Closing his eyes, he prayed his death wouldn't be painful.

Chapter One

"Was he out of his mind? Are you?" Katie Lynn Ross crouched slightly to peer through the peeling wrought-iron gate in front of her. "That's not a picturesque New England house up there—it's spook central." She scratched at the rusty bars. "Someone's playing a Halloween prank on you, Bella. And don't start with the ancestral thing. Contrary to Grandma Corrigan's belief, the children of her bloodline are not mortal links to the spirit world and therefore drawn to areas where such specters appear. This is David's idea of a final joke. Places like Darkwood Manor don't exist."

"Unless we're sharing a hallucination—unlikely—yes, they do." Going down on one knee, Isabella Ross snapped several pictures of the distant house. "Apparently."

"You're visualizing a shriveled-up corpse, aren't you? Some creepy-bird lover's mommy, stuffed and propped in the attic."

"Cellar." Isabella stopped snapping. "And what I'm imagining is the kind of hatchet job David would have done if he hadn't driven his car over that cliff last month." The sadness that swept through her brought a sigh. "I just wish he were alive so someone could talk him out of it."

Katie cast her a shrewd look. "Someone you, or someone else?"

Standing, Isabella shouldered her camera strap. "David

and I were done. It wasn't the worst breakup, but it wasn't pretty, either." She studied the vaguely Gothic structure at the end of the driveway. "Not sure why he left this place to me, but he did, so there you are. Grandma C's delighted on a visceral level while Grandpa C and Aunt Mara have dollar signs in their eyes."

"Don't you love the dynamics of a family business?"

Isabella smiled. "Actually, I do."

"Well, hell, so would I if I got to search out and develop prospective hotel sites. I crunch numbers, Bella. My job's not as glamorous as yours."

"It is when you get to descend unannounced on one of our hotels for the express purpose of exposing an embezzler."

"Yeah, that is kind of cool." Her cousin tapped out and lit a cigarette. "But are you telling me you had no inkling that David was going to leave you his—ha, ha—country house?"

"Nope. All I know is I got this place, and some distant blood relative got the rest."

"Lucky relative." Katie rattled the bars. "At a guess, I'd say your ex was worth at least…uh, okay." She released her grip as the gate stuttered inward. "I suppose this means *welcome*."

"Or *run* if we're smart?"

Katie drew a triangle with her cigarette. "Sherlock, Watson, Baskerville Hall, aka Darkwood Manor."

The gate gave an ominous creak. Not exactly a warm welcome, but Isabella was used to that. The people she met in her line of work weren't always eager to part with the structures her family wished to acquire.

Leaves swirled by a strong breeze blew around her booted ankles, and for the first time since the reading of her ex-boyfriend's will, a shiver danced along her spine. It wasn't so much a sense of foreboding, she realized, as a feeling of uncertainty.

David Gimbel had possessed many odd qualities, with quirky riding high on the list. Why he'd left her this recently purchased property in Maine might not make particular sense, but the intrigue factor far outweighed any doubts she might have. And Isabella was nothing if not easily intrigued. Her cousin—not so much.

During the walk from gate to front door, Katie bombarded her with questions. What had David planned to do with the multiwinged monstrosity before them? When had he purchased it? And again, why had he left it to Isabella rather than one of his much-despised stepsiblings?

"Face it, Bella, if a person wanted to get back at an evil step, what better way to do it than by leaving him or her a white elephant that I swear no one except maybe Edgar Allan Poe would call home?"

"So Baskerville Hall's become the House of Usher, huh?" She made a crushing motion with her foot as she spoke.

With a last deep drag, Katie ditched her cigarette. "If this place had turrets and a tower, I'd call it Dracula's castle. I can see the possibilities, though—if only from your and Grandpa C's perspective. A hoard of contractors, electricians, plumbers, painters and cleaners later, you might make a lifestyle hotel out of this. Or to use Aunt Mara's preferred term—a boutique hotel. Although why any sane person would go for Early American Gothic on vacation is…"

"Yes, I get it." Isabella surveyed the grimy windows of the second and third floors. "You won't be booking a room here."

A reluctant smile crossed Katie's lips. "Book a room on two, and you'll wind up on one. Unless you're a ghost and you can float over floorboards that are bound to be rotted through."

Isabella gave her head an amused shake. "Your glass isn't half-empty, it's bone dry."

"Only until I get back from Bangor. Once I light into those hotel ledgers, my glass'll be overflowing. Maybe I'll quit smoking for good, give you and Aunt Mara a mid-October Christmas present."

"We nag you because we love you, Katie." Isabella gave the support beam at the base of the porch a tentative poke. "Not sure about this." However, when her finger didn't penetrate, she set her foot on the first tread. It groaned but held.

A gust of wind sent a scatter of leaves across the sagging stoop, and caused a tattered screen to flap like bat wings. The shadows shifted accordingly.

Scraping her midlength hair into a stubby tail, Katie offered a flat, "So my vision won't be obscured."

"Did I ask?" Isabella regarded the cockeyed double doors. "We might need a battering ram to get inside." Backing up, she snapped another picture. "For the photo wall."

"That'll be some fun wall." Katie glanced skyward. "Why is it getting dark at three in the afternoon?"

"Because there's a storm brewing?"

"Now there's a promising answer."

Isabella inserted her key and twisted the ancient lever. To her surprise, the door moved. Only ten inches, but there was room for them to squeeze inside.

"The lawyer said it was wired," she remarked over her shoulder.

"By Thomas Edison?"

Isabella flicked the first switch she spied while Katie ventured in deeper. When a bare bulb crackled overhead, she smiled at her cousin. "Original fixtures to match the original plaster falling from the ruins of a coffered ceiling."

"And a six-inch layer of dust on every visible surface."

Katie yelped as her ankle turned on a piece of broken board. "The word *visible* not being applicable to the floor. This isn't a project, it's a death trap."

"It has good bones, though." Isabella zeroed in on the staircase. "That banister's spectacular. Carved mahogany." She took two shots. "The newel post's some kind of leaf and vine depiction. And don't say poison oak."

"I was thinking hawthorn, Bella." Katie caught her arm. "You can't seriously plan to stay here."

If this was the habitable section David's lawyer had mentioned, even Isabella wasn't that adventurous.

When her cell phone rang, she answered with a preoccupied "Isabella Ross. Hi, Aunt Mara… Yes, we're here…. Uh, well, it's—"

"Amityville," Katie declared. "And I'm being generous."

A protracted creak overhead had both women raising their eyes.

"Not sure—maybe," Isabella allowed in response to her aunt's question about ghosts. She squinted into a cobwebbed corner. "Either that or a really big rat."

"Like there's a difference?" Several yards away, Katie blew on a carved molding, then stood back, triumphant. "Behold your resident gargoyle, Bella, trapped in a sea of hemlock."

Grinning, Isabella returned to her call. "It gets better the deeper you go inside, Mara, which suggests a secondary entrance." A parlor drew her forward—until she caught a movement on the floor. "I'll get back to you when I've seen the rest." Slapping her phone closed, she dropped it in her pocket. With a wary eye on the rubble to her left she hopped onto a length of rolled carpet. "Why is there always a snake?" she muttered, shivering. "Katie, can you hear me?"

A branch scraping the window was her only response.

"Oh, good, so it's you and me, snake, and I'm betting you're poisonous." She backed along the dusty roll until it ran out. "Katie?"

Her cousin didn't reply.

Spying the movement again, Isabella gauged the distance between her and the stairwell. Grandpa Corrigan said she should face her fears. No problem, she could do that. She'd face the spot where she'd seen the snake from the far side of the entry hall.

She glanced over her shoulder. It wasn't in Katie's nature to play games. If her cousin wasn't answering, that meant she couldn't hear, ergo, she'd probably left the house for a smoke.

Still walking backward, Isabella retraced her steps to the front door.

"Going on a diet tomorrow," she decided, squeezing through. "Katie, are you out here?"

But there was no one on the porch or in the weed-choked yard. And nothing to see or hear except gusts of wind, a sky full of purplish clouds and several thick branches pressed against the windows to her right.

"Terrific," she murmured and ran the list of possibilities.

Katie never smoked indoors, so, yes, she'd have come out here to light up. But she wouldn't leave the property without a word, and they'd only been apart for a few minutes, so she couldn't have gone far. On the other hand, the floor inside was a minefield of rubble and broken furniture. She might have ventured into a room, tripped and hit her head.

Isabella slid damp palms along the sides of her pants. Grandpa C swore snakes wouldn't bite unless distressed. But then Grandpa C had marched up to and fearlessly across enemy lines numerous times in the Korean War. His idea of danger varied greatly from that of his granddaughter.

Easing back inside, she hung her shoulder bag and camera on the newel post and started for the room with the carved molding. It wasn't a gargoyle as Katie had suggested, but an angel, one with vacant orbs for eyes and an expression that sent an unexpected chill fluttering over her skin.

Because the space ahead was shuttered, she had to feel for a wall switch. A weak light appeared at the far end of the room. Directly ahead, however, the shadows remained virtually impenetrable.

"Not quite so much to love about my job at the moment," she reflected, then raised her voice. "Katie, can you hear me?"

Something shifted behind her, and she spun. But there was no one in the doorway or beyond that in the entry hall.

Exasperated by her overreaction, she regrouped and made her way carefully along the wall.

Wind whistled through cracks in the shutters. A branch banged against the siding at random intervals. The floorboards sagged and protested.

Ahead of her, a chunk of plaster toppled from a mound she could barely make out. Next to it, she spied what looked like a huddled body.

Her heart spiked. Keeping her hand on the wall and her sights fixed, she approached it.

A door at the far end of the room creaked, causing her to look up.

She realized her mistake instantly. With her concentration thrown forward, she had no time to react when her foot landed on air—and her momentum sent her tumbling into the blackness below.

FROM THE SHELTER OF a damaged shutter, the man outside watched the woman inside stumble and fall. Served her right, he thought, twitching an irritable shoulder. Now maybe she'd leave.

He couldn't do business with a snoopy female hanging around. Bad enough that big galloot from the coach house kept tromping around the perimeter of the property. With luck, he'd topple off a cliff and, if she didn't die here, take the blonde and her camera with him. Maybe some clever third person could make that happen.

On the other hand, he might not be thinking this through quite right. Lose the woman, lose the chase rabbit. Was that the best-case scenario for him?

A slow grin lit his face and made his black eyes glitter. Bad luck for the rabbit might be a lucky stroke for him. Let the woman be the focus, the diversion, the target. Leave him free to go about his business.

As he melted into the thickening twilight, the man found himself hoping the pretty blonde rabbit wouldn't die too soon.

ISABELLA'S MIND REELED. What kind of moron put a single step in the middle of whatever this room was? Ballroom, grand hall, dining room? More to the point, why hadn't she brought a flashlight from the car?

As her vision cleared and the pain of her hands-and-knees landing receded, the shape ahead resolved itself into a filthy tarp. Which relieved her because it wasn't Katie and set her nerves back on edge because there was still no sign of her cousin.

An obvious thought occurred as she pushed herself upright. Katie never went anywhere without her cell phone.

She pulled out her own cell phone and punched in Katie's number. Waited. Hissed at the pain in her left ankle when she stood, then reminded herself she deserved it for not paying attention to her surroundings.

Four rings later, Katie's voice mail picked up. Frustrated, Isabella left a message, closed her phone and, walking carefully, picked her way to the back of the room.

The door to her left stood ajar. It screeched like an angry crow when she moved it. As she crossed the threshold, she told herself the feeling of being watched came from her mind, not from the premature darkness that had begun to spread throughout the house.

Beyond the weathered walls, purple clouds had given way to brooding black, and she could hear the wind picking up. The first raindrops hit the windows as she started along a dusty corridor toward—what else—another door.

A veritable maze of interconnecting hallways, the ground floor seemed to go on forever. She passed through two kitchens, a pantry, a massive library, three dining rooms and a dozen other spaces whose purposes eluded her.

Part of her could visualize Darkwood Manor as a Corrigan-Ross property, but a much larger part was struggling with the certain knowledge that Katie wouldn't have ventured in this deep alone.

Spotting a thin door, she wedged it open. Uneven stairs topped by a rickety wooden railing descended from dusky shadow into fathomless black. *Welcome to the cellar,* she realized. *Yuck.*

Hesitating, she tapped her fingers on the jamb, then hit the light switch. "I can't think of a single reason why you'd be down there, Katie, but on the off chance you've lost your mind, I'll check it out. And be really pissed off if I find you."

From a point far below, she detected a scrape, possibly a trace of smoke. When she leaned forward, a moaning floorboard blotted the sound out, but she knew what she'd heard, and it hadn't been the foundation settling.

A bulb at the bottom provided only a weak wash of light,

barely enough to make out the mud floor. Although the stairs looked sturdier than the railing, she'd encountered dry rot before and fully anticipated it here. Still, what choice did she have?

She set her foot on the first step. When it didn't splinter, she moved to the next. And the next.

Her scraped palm stung against the stone wall. Her breath wanted to hitch. She wouldn't let it, but couldn't stop the prickles that raced over her skin.

"Not going to freak," she promised herself. "Just please don't let it be a snake pit down—"

She broke off, sucking in a startled breath as the handrail and one of the treads cracked in tandem.

Her foot shot through the plank, forcing her to grab the portion of railing still attached to the wall. That it held surprised her—but not as much as the arm that hooked her waist and hauled her upright before her trapped ankle snapped in two.

For a moment, Isabella's head swam. Then her brain clicked in and she swung her head to face a man. Possibly young. Definitely strong.

He smelled good, she noted, like soap and skin and the rain outside. While she couldn't make out his features, she spied the glimmer in his eyes.

"You don't want to go down there, Ms. Ross."

Suspicion crowded out fear. "Who are you? How do you know my name?"

"Doesn't matter."

"It does to me." She pushed on his arm. When he refused to release her, she twisted sideways. "Look, I appreciate the rescue, but I'm fine now, and I really don't have time to play games."

Instead of slackening his grip, he drew her closer until

his mouth moved against her temple. "Best use of that time you don't have would be to get in your car and leave."

She gave him a determined shove. "I'd love to if you'd let me go."

"Stop squirming and listen. You need to go back to Boston. No questions, no detours, just get on the highway and drive."

When she continued to struggle, he used the fingers of his other hand to capture her chin. "Do it, Isabella. Now. While you can." Then he drew her closer still, set his mouth next to her ear and added a soft, "If you want to live, you need to get as far away from this house as possible."

Chapter Two

He vanished before she could question him further. Vanished as he'd been trained to do by the government. As he'd been able to do long before anyone had thought to train him.

He knew the melodrama hadn't worked. He hadn't expected it would. But short of tying a blanket over her head and tossing her on a southbound train, it was the best he could manage.

He wasn't supposed to be in the house. He'd promised his uncle he would look around discreetly, without fuss. Fuss led to attention, and that would send the rats scurrying.

If they'd been ordinary rats, he wouldn't have cared. He still wasn't sure why he did, but his uncle was concerned, so it wouldn't hurt him to skulk for a while.

If it turned out Haden was right, something should probably be done. Maybe by him, maybe by someone else. The who here depended on how the local authorities reacted to a hot blonde in a long, black leather coat, with skin that shouted peaches and cream and eyes so blue he'd been struck by the color fifty feet away.

The woman had courage. He admired that. She was determined, likely stubborn. Couldn't fault those qualities. She also had a body under that black coat…

Blanking his mind to the fantasy, he watched her from his crouch on the sheltered side of the house.

Purposeful strides carried her along the driveway to the front gate and through it to the other side. She didn't use an umbrella, and she didn't bother to belt her coat. She had the shoulder bag he'd rifled, her 2K camera and, he imagined, an expression on her face that matched her body language.

A reluctant smile tugged on his lips the longer he watched her. Too bad nothing would come of it, but then he was used to nothing, and what he did have—primarily his uncle—more than compensated for the lack.

Her car engine roared. The tires spit wet gravel as she turned it toward Mystic Harbor, Maine, a town where he and more than one of his ancestors had been born.

His name was Donovan Black. Like it or not—and he definitely did not—he was connected to Darkwood Manor. Which was why, no matter how tempting Ms. Isabella Ross might be, he would never be connected to her.

"YOU'RE NOT GOING TO do anything, are you?" Isabella stared down at a thirtysomething man with a crooked nose and very large teeth. "You have more important matters to attend to than searching for a woman, a stranger, that no one, including you or your deputies, has seen. In any case, Darkwood Manor is situated on the fringe of your jurisdiction, so maybe she's crossed the county line by now. Problem solved. Have a nice night, ma'am."

The man's smile didn't falter. "Could be you're right there, Ms. Ross. Could also be you're inventing a crime to drum up publicity for a new hotel."

Exasperation won out. "That's ridiculous. My family doesn't stoop to publicity stunts. We go about things the old-fashioned way. We advertise. And we only do that when a hotel is up and running. Not only is Darkwood Manor not in that category, it isn't even a hotel."

"Yet."

Isabella held fast to her Irish temper. "Sheriff Lucas, I've had a really crappy afternoon. I'm not asking you to launch a full-scale search for Katie, I just want you to take a few minutes and look into her disappearance."

"Can't do much in a few minutes, now can I, Blondie?"

"Excuse me?"

"Sorry. Ms. Ross." His smirk belied the apology. "Now, I've been patient, and I've listened to your story with an open mind."

So open, Isabella thought, that it had drained from his head.

"You say you and your cousin drove up here this afternoon from Boston."

"I said we drove up from Portland."

"Via Portland, but you live and work in Boston. You also said you came here then drove to Darkwood in separate vehicles. Why is that exactly?"

Isabella refused to let him rattle her composure. "I've already explained. Katie was going on to Bangor. I was stopping here. Two destinations, two vehicles."

"And your cousin's vehicle, like your cousin herself, is currently unaccounted for?"

"Yes."

"That doesn't suggest anything to you?"

Her eyes narrowed to dangerous slits. "It suggests that both Katie and her car are missing."

The sheriff's smile grew strained. "A stronger suggestion would be that something at Darkwood Manor spooked her. When she couldn't find you, she gave in to her fear and ran."

"She's not answering her cell phone."

"Maybe she dropped it in her rush to escape. People have been known to leave all manner of personal possessions behind as they scramble back through those gates. Don't get me wrong, I'm not a believer myself, but more than a few folks hereabouts swear the manor's haunted."

"Oh, good." Isabella mustered a false smile. "Here comes the ghost story. Katie wasn't spirited away, Sheriff, and she didn't run out on me."

"You think someone kidnapped her and stole her car."

"I think that's a more plausible explanation than believing she ran from a ghost."

Yet, in spite of herself, her conviction wavered. To bolster it, she jammed her hands in the pockets of her coat. "Whose spirit is supposed to haunt the place?"

"Take your pick. Aaron Dark, builder and owner. Aaron's wife, Sybil, who ran off with another man. The unborn child some swear she was carrying. Hell, it could be Dark's sister took up residence after she died, as penance for having her brother locked away."

"Interesting. But you don't believe any of those stories, so it can't be fear that's stopping you from driving out there with me."

He gave her an insulting once-over. "Do you drink, Ms. Ross?"

She wouldn't react, she told herself, would not lose it because some pasty-faced sheriff was either too lazy or too jittery to help her.

So instead of answering his question, she tipped her head to the side. "Tell me, Sheriff Lucas, is there something untoward going on at Darkwood Manor? Some illegal activity that might necessitate Katie's removal from the house and cause me to be warned off?"

The sheriff's open mouth closed with a snap. "You didn't mention that you were warned off."

"You didn't give me a chance, and I'm mentioning it now."

"Who did the warning?"

"I have no idea. A man on the cellar stairs. He told me to leave Darkwood Manor and not come back."

The smile returned. "There you go, then. He probably told your cousin the same thing. Only unlike you, she took his advice."

"At a dead run. Dropping her cell phone in the process. And since then, hasn't bothered to stop and contact me. She wouldn't do that, Sheriff—as I've already said."

"What did this man of yours look like?"

"Again, no idea. He stopped me from falling down the cellar stairs, told me to leave and disappeared. If you won't help me find Katie, you could at least help me track down this mystery man. It's possible he saw what happened to her, and that's why he warned me to leave."

The sheriff's brow furrowed. Rain streaming over the station windows gave his face a streaky look, as if it were melting.

When he didn't speak, Isabella tried one last time to reason with him. "Sheriff Lucas, all I'm asking—"

"Is that I drive out to a deserted house with inadequate lighting in search of tire marks that will have long since washed away—if they ever existed—to look for a woman and or a mystery man that only you saw and or heard, and in the process risk breaking my neck the way you almost did in broad daylight."

Isabella's eyes glittered. "I take it that's a no."

"On all counts." Rolling back from his desk, he stood. "Your cousin doesn't contact you by tomorrow, I might have one of my deputies take a drive out there with you. If she shows, you're welcome to come in and apologize for jabbering at me over nothing when I should be home eating my wife's crab cakes and helping my kid with his algebra. Hotel charges eighty bucks a night off-season. Turn left at the end of Harbor Road if you're looking for the highway.

Your choice, Ms. Ross. You have a good night one way or the other."

To Isabella's astonishment, instead of ushering her out, he snatched his raincoat from a peg, crushed his hat down onto his head and stalked through the door of the small station house.

She stood there for a moment, stunned, until a thread of humor slithered in.

"Okay, then. No worries to you, too, pal. And apparently none to whoever's in your cell block."

Because there was definitely someone snoring away in the back. Whether deputy or prisoner, however, she didn't care. Bottom line? Lucas was an ass. And he wasn't going to help her find Katie.

Following the sheriff's lead, Isabella let herself out. The street was virtually dead. The rain had let up and fog had moved in, a great swirling bank of it. Water droplets plopped onto the sidewalk behind her. To her left, a woman's high heels tapped in the opposite direction.

She thought about the hotel across the street. Their brochures read Come Inn to the Mystic, which would have been a good tagline if the place hadn't been a cardboard cutout of every generic hotel in rural America.

Oh, there was plenty of room for competition in this town.

Jingling her keys, she turned for her car.

"No assistance to be had, Ms. Ross?"

The silence was so pervasive, it made the words, spoken from the fog in front of her, sound like cannon fire. But even with her heart in her throat, Isabella's restraint held.

"The ghost thing won't work on me. I'm not in the mood for games, and I'm not leaving, so if you're planning a repeat performance of our cellar staircase encounter, you can save your breath. My cousin was here. Now she's not. I'm going to find her. End of conversation."

"I didn't take her, Isabella."

"Yes, I reasoned that one out, although given the circumstances, it's possible you came to my assistance at Darkwood Manor to throw me off."

Amusement colored his tone. "You're being too clever, and giving me way more credit for that quality than I deserve. I told you to leave because a man I trust insists there's something going on at the manor. Since he's not prone to hallucinations, there probably is. Hidden agendas frequently go hand in hand with crime."

"Spoken like a true cop." When he didn't respond, she arched her brows. "Would that be a silent confirmation or the silent voice of criminal experience?"

"Possibly a little of both."

That did it. Yes, the man had a great voice. She liked the way he smelled, and what she'd seen of his eyes in the cellar had mesmerized her for a moment. But her love of a good mystery paled next to her concern for Katie's life. So...

She took a challenging step forward. "Did you go through my purse or my car to find out who I am?"

"I didn't see your car until later. Your purse was hanging at the bottom of the stairs."

"My stairs, Mr...."

"Black. Donovan. And I'm aware that you own Darkwood Manor."

"So you are a cop."

"Of sorts."

"Friends with the local sheriff?"

"Good friends."

Why that surprised her, she couldn't say, but as long as it was there, she might as well seize the opportunity. "In that case, would you do me a favor?"

"I might."

"All I want—"

"Is for me to persuade the sheriff to search for your cousin."

"Which you won't do because…?"

Again, the suggestion of a smile. "Sheriff's in Florida, recovering from a gunshot wound to the chest. The man you talked to is his replacement, Senior Deputy, aka acting sheriff, Ormand Lucas. Genuine-article sheriff won't be back until after Halloween."

Pressing the fingers of both hands to her temples, Isabella murmured a disbelieving "Remind me to get my Aunt Rose to put a curse on this town." She dropped her hands. "Let's cut the small talk, okay? How do you even know about my cousin? Did you see us at Darkwood Manor?"

"I saw you. Searching for your cousin there and talking to Orry here."

"So you eavesdropped through a closed door."

"From the back room. Mystic Harbor's a small town, less than a thousand residents at this time of year. Alley doors are seldom locked. Have you had dinner?"

Was he joking? She squared up. "Why are you hiding in the dark, Mr. Black?"

"I'm not hiding, I'm leaning on a lamppost having a conversation with a beautiful woman. Dinner?"

Part of her wanted to laugh. The rest… "It might have escaped your notice, but I've had a few more important things on my mind. Katie wasn't spirited away by the ghost of Aaron Dark. She didn't bolt in fear or lose her cell phone, and she doesn't play practical jokes. She's gone, her car's gone, and your soon-to-be-cursed acting sheriff couldn't care less about any of it. Forget food. My question is, as a cop of sorts, are you going to get involved or not?"

"I'm thinking about it."

It was more than she'd expected, but not enough for her to trust him. "Okay, second question." She waved at the fog, thought she could almost make out a figure in the darkness ahead. "Am I ever going to see you?"

She knew he hesitated. However, after a few seconds, a man wearing a black coat similar to hers emerged.

He was taller than her, but no more than six feet or so in boots. Worn jeans were topped by a black T. He had good hands, she noted, and surprisingly long hair. Far too long for your average cop. It was mid-brown, shoulder length and somehow sensual. His face intrigued her, too. More than nice, but not quite remarkable, his features were nonetheless riveting.

Then she saw his eyes, and both her assessment and the breath in her lungs stalled.

"Whoa." She reacted unthinkingly, paused, then drew back. "You have great eyes." It took a few seconds for her brain to roll with the sexual punch, longer still to recall what they'd been saying. When she did, she moved a finger between them. "You mentioned something about dinner?"

His slow smile almost caused a full meltdown, but this time she was prepared for it and braced.

"I know a place," he said. "We can talk there, maybe strategize to some extent. How much will be up to you."

"Why me?"

His smile widened. "You might not like the company."

"We're having company?"

"One other person."

"Ah. Would that be your wife, Mr. Black?"

"Uncle. I'm not married. And it's Donovan."

"Okay, Donovan. Why should your uncle, or any other man, affect our conversation?"

"He shouldn't." Donovan turned her around. "As long as you're not afraid of bears."

HADEN BLACK WASN'T A bear. Not quite. Bigfoot was closer, but even legendary beasts had claws. Donovan's uncle had potholders. And bifocals. And a rustic cottage crammed to the rafters with reading material, art and vintage electronics.

She counted three televisions, two turntables, a serious sound system, a reel-to-reel tape deck and the worn covers of at least a thousand LPs.

The man stood a burly six feet seven inches, sported a bushy beard and had a wild head of hair that skimmed his massive shoulders. He spoke in a growl, looked like he could bench press her weight and Donovan's combined, and made no attempt to disguise his contempt for her ex.

"The man was a fool with more money than brains. Said he wanted to turn the manor into a spa." Although he didn't spit, she sensed he wanted to. "Sweet-talked the geezer who owned it into selling for a song."

To hide her amusement, Isabella glanced away. Then did a double take and knelt to regard an abstract canvas carelessly propped against a stack of logs. "David's partner said he paid over nine hundred thousand for the place. Is this a Kandinsky?"

"You've got good eyes." Haden grunted his approval. "No taste in men, though. Nine hundred thousand's peanuts for a cliffside manor with acreage. Tell her, Donovan."

"It's worth more," his nephew agreed. At Isabella's upward glance, he chuckled. "That being said, the transaction was legal and probably fair enough, considering the owner just celebrated his ninety-third birthday, has been predeceased by all his heirs and planned to put the place on the market for less than half of what your boyfriend paid."

"Former boyfriend." Isabella tipped another canvas forward, stared in disbelief. "You have a Van Gogh?"

"Got a Picasso kicking around somewhere, too."

"On the floor."

Haden shot her an aggravated look. "No room for 'em on the walls now, is there. Tell me, Ms. Corrigan-Ross, what are your plans for the house?"

Standing, she dusted off. "To tear it apart piece by cracked plaster piece until I find my cousin. My name's Isabella. And I think your dinner's burning, Mr. Black."

"Haden." He shook a potholder at her. "Are you one hundred percent sure this cousin of yours didn't turn tail and run because something scared her?"

"Something as in Aaron Dark's ghost?"

He set belligerent fists on his hips. "Are you a nonbeliever, then?"

She summoned a placid smile. "My grandparents on both sides are Irish. I have to buy in to some extent."

"But?" Donovan prompted.

"My father's father was a hardcore New York businessman. His mother was a city councillor. Ghosts don't exist in their world, even in theory. So to answer your question, when asked, I tend to take the Fifth."

"You sound like a politician."

"You sound like my grandma Corrigan."

"Woman has sense." Haden shook the potholder again. "Hang around here long enough, you'll believe in spooks, spirits, poltergeists and probably Elvis come back from the grave."

"If you're saying I'm going to bump into Aaron Black at some point in my search, good. When I do, maybe he'll help me find Katie."

"Don't count on it," Donovan said behind her. "Aaron Dark wasn't the helpful sort."

Prepared for the sexual punch, Isabella faced him. "You know, for a cop, you're awfully cryptic."

"He's a sharpshooter." Haden headed for the now-smoking oven. "Boy has the best eyes in the business."

No argument there, she thought. However, it was the Aaron Dark reference that interested her. "The notes David left with his partner spoke of a philanthropic man, active in politics, the business community and the local church."

"The details of which were neatly set down in the family history." Donovan's lips curved. "What wasn't mentioned anywhere in those notes was that Aaron Dark wrote the bulk of that history. Other, less biased accounts suggest a Jekyll and Hyde personality."

She smiled. "That would just make for a more colorful story."

"It would, unless you had dealings with him."

Curiosity had her studying his expression. That and she couldn't drag her gaze from his face. "Are you a history buff, then, Donovan?"

He glanced away, smiled a little. "Nothing quite so easy."

"You just love a good ghost story, huh?"

"A good one, yes. Unfortunately, this story isn't." He came closer, kept his eyes locked on hers. "Aaron Dark was a monster, Isabella. He imprisoned his wife at Darkwood Manor. When he discovered she was pregnant with another man's child, he killed her and threw her body from the cliff behind the house."

Although something about his demeanor had changed, Isabella couldn't have said what it was. "Pretty sure none of that was in David's notes. Was Dark arrested? Hung? Run out of town?"

"He went mad," Donovan told her. She swore his brown eyes deepened to black. "And to answer your unspoken question, I know that because Aaron Dark's sister, his sister who many believe went as mad as Aaron, was my ancestor."

Chapter Three

If he'd intended to shock her—and he probably had—the attempt fell flat. Her eyes danced as she curled a finger around the front of his shirt. "Second reminder, pal. Someday I'll tell you about my ancestor Connell Ross who went on a bloody post-death rampage after his land was gutted by an enemy army that, like every army in the dark days of Ireland's history, decided to make what was his, theirs. Long story short, anyone who tries to build on Connell's land is doomed to failure. We all have our skeletons, Donovan. Some are just more recently formed than others."

Haden was no help. The smug "Told you so" that wafted out of the kitchen made Isabella laugh and Donovan want to say to hell with both of them and return to his life in New York.

He liked living on the edge; he'd lived there for most of his thirty-six years. The way he saw it, if he didn't explore the dark side of his nature, he'd never know how deep his ancestral tendencies ran. Or so the childhood theory went.

He was spared the necessity of a reply when his uncle marched in with two heaping platters of food and a bottle of wine.

As it turned out, the meat was only slightly charred. A Cordon Bleu chef, Haden set a table bountiful enough to feed half the population of Mystic Harbor. To her credit, recognizable or not, Isabella sampled every dish, and only seemed mildly puzzled by the meat.

"This isn't rabbit, is it?"

Busy chewing, Haden shook his head, motioned for her to eat and nudged the arugula-and-anchovy salad closer to her plate.

The lights above them flickered. The big man swallowed, stood. "Leave room for dessert," he warned and clomped out to check the fuse box.

Spearing a piece of meat, Isabella lifted it for a closer inspection. "Why do I think this never had feathers?"

Donovan kept his expression neutral. "It's squirrel."

Her eyes came up. "Squirrel," she repeated. Her fork went down. "As in Rocky the Flying?"

"Or a close relative." Resting his forearms on the table, he snagged a bottle. "More wine?"

"I fed peanuts to park squirrels when I was growing up."

"If you can eat Thumper and Chicken Little, Isabella, why a problem with Rocky?"

Still staring, she moved her glass forward. "I was being polite. I prefer not to eat any of them. I'll be a little more rude next time." Ignoring the lights that surged and faded overhead, she slid her gaze to his face. "Insanity isn't an inherited trait, you know."

He swirled his wine, swallowed a bitter mouthful. "Do you want to tell my mother that, or leave it to the doctors who are treating her?"

"For what?"

"Paranoia mostly, with a little ADHD thrown in on the side. And then there was my grandmother who, depending on which day of the week it happened to be, saw herself as Eleanor Roosevelt, Mary Pickford and, toward the end of her life, Anna McNeill Whistler."

"Your grandmother thought she was Whistler's mother?"

"Until the day she died. She wanted to be buried in North Carolina, where Anna was born. During a rare moment of lucidity, my mother denied the request and had her remains interred in the family crypt."

Isabella set her chin on a fisted hand. "You're going to tell me I own the crypt, aren't you?"

"Inasmuch as anyone can own such a thing."

"What about this place? I heard it was the coach house for the manor."

"It was, but you don't own it. The cottage sits in the middle of the only acre of land the Darks held on to when the manor was sold early in the twentieth century. The buyer was a shipbuilder from Portland. Your ex bought it, sans acre, from the last of the builder's descendants."

"Well, I'm fascinated." She pushed her plate away as the lights winked off and on. "Does this disco ball effect happen a lot?"

Donovan took another sip. "Haden rewired the place last year. Answer's yes." When she continued her speculative regard, he let his lips curve, considered the wine in his glass. "Something else?"

"I'm not sure." Leaning in on her forearms, she twirled a strand of his hair around her finger. "You're a strange sort of cop, Donovan Black. And don't say it runs in the family."

He let her touch, made a point of not lowering his gaze to the vee of her dark red sweater. "It doesn't," he answered. "I'm an aberration in that regard."

"In lots of regards, I imagine."

"With one exception."

She gave his hair a tug. "Nice try, Black, but my uncle's a Park Avenue shrink. Insanity doesn't walk, run or gallop in families."

"A shrink, huh?" Even knowing he shouldn't, Donovan

found himself wanting to sample her mouth. One brief taste to satisfy the hunger in his belly. Then he'd remove himself from the moment and from temptation. From Mystic Harbor as well, if he was smart—which he could be or not, depending on the situation.

The lights dimmed again. He heard Haden swearing on the back porch, but his eyes remained on Isabella. On her soft, striking features, her long, rain-curled hair and her bluer-than-blue eyes.

He wasn't sure who actually moved, but he figured it was probably fifty-fifty. However it happened, his mouth was suddenly on hers, not to taste now, but to dive in and explore.

Catching her jaw between his thumb and fingers, he angled her head to deepen the kiss. She made a sound of approval in her throat, tangled her own fingers in his hair and pulled him closer.

At their first meeting, she'd shoved him away. He should have left it at that. Left her to face whatever demons lurked inside Darkwood Manor alone. Instead, his tongue was on a voyage of discovery in her mouth, fencing with hers, then sliding past it, until the pulse hammering in his head threatened to strip away decades of control.

When the lights above them sparked, a red warning flashed in his brain. If it looked and felt dangerous, it probably was. Even as he tested the limits of his restraint, Donovan knew he should end this now, walk away and not look back.

He wasn't sure if he could have done it or not. The next time the lights zapped off, they stayed that way, plunging the cottage into full, silent darkness. He let her bite his bottom lip, was thinking about trailing his mouth along the side of her neck when they heard it—a long, keening wail that echoed through the fog and shadow outside.

It started on the periphery of his mind and built, from a thread of sound to a shriek that had Isabella's fingernails sinking into his shoulders.

"My God, what is that?"

He couldn't see her clearly, but knew she was staring at the front window.

His eyes slid in the same direction. "Some people say a pack of wolves wandered down from Quebec. A few think it's a wild dog."

She didn't pull back, and his hand still formed a light V around her throat. "Some," she repeated. As the wail came again, he felt a shiver ripple through her. "What do the rest of the people believe?"

"What you'd expect." He kept his tone calm. "That Aaron Dark's spirit has come to reclaim his house. And if he can't get it using fear, he'll resort to what he knows best. Death."

"You know I don't buy any of that, don't you?"

They were the first words out of Isabella's mouth when Donovan halted his black Tundra behind her on the narrow roadway.

She'd been pacing in front of the Hang Ten Lodge, the only other off-season accommodations Mystic Harbor had to offer, waiting for him to join her and going over his remarks about Aaron Dark's afterlife agenda.

She didn't think he really believed in ghosts. In the possibility of genetic insanity, yes, but not in encounters with otherworldly beings.

He was trying to frighten her again, and she didn't appreciate the repeat performance one bit. Especially when her head continued to spin from a kiss like—well, like nothing she'd ever experienced before. Her lips were still tingling, and sorting through her jumbled thoughts had only become possible in the last five minutes.

Back at his place, Haden's announcement that the power outage extended beyond the walls of his cottage had barely registered.

"You must be tuckered out," he'd remarked with a sympathetic tut. "Put that sound you heard out of your mind. It's a story for later. For tonight, you go to my friend George's lodge. State it's in, the manor's not fit for flesh-and-blood humans. Last owner slept on a horsehair sofa so lumpy it makes my yard look like a putting green. We'll talk tomorrow about the goings-on up there. Meantime, I'll call ahead, tell George you're on your way."

Horsehair sofas, mad ghosts and one incredible kiss. If Katie had been a weak-minded person, Isabella might have believed she'd run. But they weren't merely cousins, they were best friends and had been since before she could remember. Katie had not left Darkwood Manor voluntarily.

Isabella kept pacing while Donovan leaned against the hood of his truck and watched.

"Ghosts, whether real or imagined, don't whisk people and their vehicles away," she maintained in passing. Cell phone in hand, she tried her cousin's number again, with the same result as before.

A frustrated sound escaped. Letting her head fall back, she surveyed the misty night sky. "I'm going to wake up soon and discover this is nothing but a nightmare. I figure there's a sixty-forty chance that no part of it's real." Bringing her head up, she regarded the rustic lodge to her left. "Why are there lights inside?"

"Generator's running. They have limited power." Locking his eyes on hers, Donovan pushed off from the hood, moved toward her with deliberation. "I wasn't trying to scare you back at Haden's place, Isabella. It was a reaction, a verbal

shove. Not a fair one, but that's how self-defense mecha-
nisms work. Anything to keep a threat at bay."

For the first time since she'd left the cottage, humor
sparked. "In other words, kissing me unnerved you."

"You could say that." His gaze didn't waver as he approached. "But a more accurate assessment would be to say
it scared the crap out of me."

"I'm flattered, Black."

"Don't be."

A chuckle emerged from the shadowed front porch. "Trust
him, he means it," a husky female voice drawled. "Hey-ya,
Donovan. What brings you to our sequestered neck of the
woods?"

Donovan's gaze remained on Isabella. "Thought you were
moving to the Cape, Darlene."

"So did I. Best-laid plans'll screw you every time. Who's
the blonde?"

Dragging her eyes from Donovan's, Isabella smiled. "Isabella Ross."

"The new owner of Darkwood Manor," Donovan supplemented.

A tall, thin woman came into the misty half-light. She
had an unlit cigarette between her black-tipped fingers and
sharp, foxlike features that were neither friendly nor un-
friendly. Platinum hair stood up like frosted candy canes,
she wore a rock-band T beneath an oversized leather jacket
and studded boots over superskinny jeans.

"Darlene Calvert." She gestured at the building behind
her. "My mother and Donovan's are tenth or twelfth cousins.
Means we're related, but hey, life sucks on lots of levels. You
looking for a room?"

Unsure what to make of her, Isabella offered a cautious
"Maybe. Is this your lodge?"

Darlene snorted, struck a match, inhaled.

"It's her mother's," Donovan said.

"Only a masochistic fool would want to rent rooms to the public." She adopted a whiny tone. "The bed's too hard, the food's too cold, the bathroom's too small. Goldilocks should have been so picky." She lowered spiky lashes. "So, what's your line, Isabella?"

"Apparently I'm a masochistic fool."

"Hotel worker?"

"My family's in the business."

"Ross, huh?" A sly smile appeared. "As in the Corrigan-Ross Hotel Group? And now you're eyeing Darkwood Manor as a destination for supernatural thrill seekers." She blew a line of smoke. "Sweetie, if that's your intention, you wanna scuttle it here and now."

"Why would I do that, Darlene?"

The woman strolled closer, let her gaze travel in the direction of the distant manor. "Because I drove past your recent acquisition this afternoon. Saw a man at the gate."

"What did he look like?" Isabella asked with care.

"Tall, thirtysomething, dark haired, might have had a 'stache. I stopped for a moment, because—well, because I was curious. I shouldn't have, though. I could tell, not sure how, that he wanted me to keep moving."

"Did he speak to you?"

"No, he just glared."

"And then?"

"Then he started walking toward me. He came through the gate and headed straight for my car. That's when I took off."

With Katie missing, Isabella had no time for theatrics. "Did you feel threatened by him?"

"You could say that." Blowing more smoke, Darlene sliced a hand in front of her. "I said he came through the gate. Thing is, the gate was closed at the time."

"I'M SUPPOSED TO BELIEVE a ghost walked through a closed gate." Isabella strode into the partially lit lodge ahead of Donovan. "The ghost glared, Darlene left and, after the shock wore off, went about her usual business." She stalked back to him. "Is she on meds, or do I just look like someone who believes in the tooth fairy?"

Donovan turned her back around. "You own Darkwood Manor, Isabella. Ghost sightings come with the territory." Setting his head next to hers, he nodded at a woman in jeans and a plaid shirt who was delivering a round of beer to a group of poker players at one of five tables strewn about the lobby. "That's George."

"Of course it is." But Isabella worked up a pleasant expression when the woman wiped her hands and came to join them.

"Haden called, said you'd be wanting a room." She pushed at a mop of salt-and-pepper hair, winked at Donovan. "Don't let these noisy hooligans losing a month's wages to each other put you off. They pay me for the space, so I let them pick each other's pockets twice a week. Sorry about the bad light, but the generator's old. I've got a room upstairs or a cabin if you'd prefer. Both come with lanterns. Cabin has a fireplace and a fridge."

Isabella's smile had a dangerous edge. "Does it have a ghost as well?"

The woman named George laughed. "Ran into Darlene outside, did you? Now, honey, you forget about her. My girl's a frustrated journalist is all. Had a job lined up south of here, but lost out to the editor's niece. She's back working for our local Realtor and being pissy about it. The cabins are clean, private and ghost free. You can see Darkwood Manor up on the cliff from number three."

Unable to sustain her irritation in the face of George's

friendly manner, Isabella relaxed. "Your lodge is lovely, and I know all about pissy moods. It's been a long day."

George squeezed her wrist. "Why don't I let Donovan show you the way. If he remembers, that is. Our boy left us right after he graduated high school. Only comes back to visit Haden and me and old Gunnar Crookshank...when the damn fool's not off recovering from a gunshot wound that wouldn't have happened if a certain deputy—Orry Lucas— had better aim."

Orry Lucas? Isabella's head swung to the tables. And there he was, half-hidden behind a rough beam, out of the main pool of light, the man she'd spoken to in town.

"Evening, Ms. Ross, Donovan. Didn't know you two were friends."

Isabella's lips tipped up. "I'd have mentioned it," she lied, "but you were so anxious to get home and help your son with his algebra that I didn't want to hold you up."

Donovan chuckled. "Algebra, Orry?"

"I was riled. I meant homework."

"Your kid's in preschool. How much homework does he have?"

"Any amount'd be over Orry's head," a man with a cigar in his mouth chortled. "Truth be told, our deputy was probably worried his wife would bean him for talking to a pretty stranger. She's a bit jealous, that one. I should know—she's my niece."

Isabella regarded Donovan, now perched on one of the empty tables. "Is everyone in this town related?"

"Mostly." He raised his voice. "Isabella's cousin's still missing, Orry. You planning to do anything about that?"

"Adults are free to come and go as they please in these parts. I'll look into it when the time's right."

Assuming he could tell time, Isabella thought, firing up.

Reading her body language, Donovan shook his head.

"Let it go. He can make himself an object of ridicule without our help."

George sniffed. "It's no more than he deserves. Oh, here's more beer coming. You think for a minute, honey. Let me know what you'd like."

Isabella ground her teeth. "A real-life sheriff would be nice." But she kept her voice low and her eyes on Donovan, who somehow managed to fit in yet be removed from his surroundings at the same time.

"Excuse me, Ms. Ross, Mr. Black." A man with slippery black hair and a prominent widow's peak approached them. He wore a white shirt, jeans and loafers, had long, narrow features and looked completely out of place in the New England lodge. "My name's Robert Drake. Deputy Lucas tells me you're in the hotel business, Ms. Ross. I built a number of town homes in Brunswick last year. I'm thinking of doing the same thing up here."

"Did the deputy also happen to mention that the lady's got herself some prime property?" Donovan asked in an easy tone.

"Property, yes. Prime's open for debate." Drake's mouth smiled; his eyes didn't. "I can't say I'd be eager to get mixed up with a ghost, and I'm told you've got a nasty one."

Isabella matched his smile. "I'll let you know when I meet him."

He raised his palms. "You've got more courage than I do. I'm not a fan of ghosts myself."

Curious, she thought, since, with his black eyes and pale skin, he resembled one.

The cigar man stabbed a finger across the table. "I'm a fan of anyone human or vapor who's got money in his pocket. Get your butt over here, Donovan, and take friggin' Orry's place, will ya? He antes up once, then folds."

"Raise the stakes," Donovan suggested.

Isabella glanced at his profile. She could see what Robert Drake probably couldn't. The developer was being thoroughly assessed, from slicked-back hair to Gucci loafer.

In a practiced move, Drake produced a card from his shirt pocket. "On the off chance you decide to part with some of your land, here's my name and number. Far from the haunted manor would be best, but that's a personal aversion. As a businessman, I try to be open-minded."

George returned to shoo him away. "The other players are waiting, and my new guest's had a long day. Cabin or room, Isabella?"

"Cabin three," Isabella decided. "I like a view."

"In that case, key's behind the desk, Donovan." George rolled her eyes as the poker player with the cigar swore. "God's sake, watch your mouth, Milt. I'm sure Isabella's not looking to color up her vocabulary."

"She won't need me to help her with that if old Aaron's on a tear," the man countered. "My first mate swears he heard the screech of the damned while we were sitting a mile off the Point last month. I was below asleep, so he chugged over to check it out. Suddenly, a Corvette shot over the cliff, crashed and burned like hellfire. And so Darkwood Manor changed hands again. I don't mean to scare you, lady, but my feeling is it'll keep changing hands until it's a Dark who owns it again."

"Or someone with Dark blood," Orry mumbled behind his cards. At Donovan's look, he showed his teeth. "Just saying."

George swatted Donovan's arm. "Rescue the poor girl, for heaven's sake."

"Actually…" Isabella began, but George cut her off.

"You let Haden tell you what you need to know. Or Donovan if he's in the mood." She swatted him again. "He won't be, but who could object to having a sexy-as-hell man evading her questions?"

Isabella thought this might be one of the most surreal evenings of her life. God knew her emotions were all over the place. She needed to collect her thoughts and regroup.

Donovan was removing the key to cabin three when her cell phone beeped. Digging it from her coat pocket, she glanced at the screen.

"What?" he asked when she stopped.

Her brow knit into a frown. "I just got a text message." She looked up at him. "From Katie."

Bella. Had to leave. Sorry. Emergency. Details ASAP. Katie.

ISABELLA ROLLED THE WORDS through her head during the walk to the cliff-side cabin. The more she rolled them, the more suspicious she became. When was the last time Katie had texted her? The word *never* sprang to mind.

"Katie's not a texter," she maintained. When Donovan didn't slow down, she caught his arm. "Did you...?"

"I heard you, Isabella. You don't believe she sent the message. Someone could have sent it for her."

"Why?"

"You know your cousin better than I do."

"Exactly. Which is why this makes no sense. If Katie did leave the manor without a word—highly unlikely—she'd have needed to drive somewhere. She could have contacted me anytime between Darkwood and her destination."

"Not if she was talking to the person who called her."

"You're being obtuse."

"I'm being a cop."

"Is there a difference?" She dug in. "This feels wrong, Donovan."

He regarded her for several seconds, then finally asked, "How many times have you tried to contact her since the message came through?"

"Four. She's not answering."

"Yeah, I got that part." He gave the latch a whack, pushed the door open and let her precede him inside.

Even after they lit a lantern, the shadows remained deep enough to rival anything Isabella had encountered at Darkwood Manor. She took in what she could of the room—a sofa with cushions and throws, a tub chair, a writing desk, some kind of table, two braided rugs on a wood floor and three closed doors. To her surprise, most of the opposite wall was comprised of windows.

The current view was shrouded in fog; however, when the layers shifted she glimpsed Darkwood Manor, looming like an evil fortress on a ragged jut of cliff. Below, she heard the relentless pounding of the surf—the sound of which momentarily diverted her.

"Why the Hang Ten Lodge?" she asked over her shoulder. "Do people actually surf in these waters?"

"Not that I know of. Ten people were hung on the spot where the lodge was built."

"Once again, it's all about death. Any of those hanged ten stick around, or am I the only one who's haunted?"

"Far as I know, you're it."

"I see. Details on that?"

His lips curved. "Haden's the details guy."

Resigned, she glanced through the bank of windows, turned, then halted and snapped her head around for a second look. "Someone's out there."

Donovan leaned over her shoulder. "Where?"

"On the cliff. Right…" She waited until the fog swirled apart. "There. At the edge of the cliff behind the manor."

The fog closed in again, like a cloud across the moon.

Isabella dipped lower. Several seconds later, the layers separated.

But while the rocks and trees remained, the figure she'd seen had vanished.

Chapter Four

Murky night fog bled into a sullen gray dawn. The low overcast gave Mystic Harbor and the cliffs surrounding it an eerie pall.

Or maybe it was his mind, Donovan reflected, re-creating a world of childhood shadows to block the all-too-harsh reality of his mother's delusions.

His uncle was snoring like a grizzly when he left the cottage. He'd already contacted a cop friend in Boston who'd promised to check out Katie Lynn Ross's cell phone records. Why he'd done it, he couldn't say, or if he could, didn't want to.

He hadn't seen the figure on the cliff, and he didn't know a damn thing about Isabella Ross except that she was beautiful, her eyes continued to haunt him and kissing her had been the biggest mistake he'd made in years.

Zipping a leather jacket over jeans and a gray T, he stuffed a gun into his waistband, capped the coffee Haden had preset to brew and hiked to the top of Darkwood Ridge.

Lingering tendrils of mist slunk around his ankles. Most of the ground was rocky, but there was the odd patch of dirt where bushes and weeds had managed to take root. Although the manor itself was crowded on two sides, trees wisely avoided the cliff. Given the storms that frequently battered this section of the coast, Donovan was amazed that one of them hadn't fallen and punched a hole in the manor's roof.

Crouching, he examined the soil and needle beds, checked the bushes for signs of breakage and the weeds to see if they'd been flattened. He was sipping his coffee when a pair of black boots came into view.

"Either your kid's taken to chewing on leather or you've got yourself a dog, Lucas. I'll go with the dog."

The deputy's feet shifted into an ornery stance. "You're trespassing, Black. I could arrest you for that."

"Do it, and see how long it takes the sheriff to relieve you of your badge."

"Until Crookshank gets back, I am the sheriff."

Donovan examined a soggy cigarette butt. "What are you doing here, Acting Sheriff?"

"Same as you, I expect, only without the perks."

"Uh-huh. How's your wife?"

"Not pining for you, if that's what you're thinking."

It wasn't, so Donovan let his gaze roam the rough edge ahead. "You don't believe her, do you?"

"Not for a minute. Ms. Isabella Corrigan hyphen Ross is looking to drum up publicity for her family's soon-to-be hotel. First she comes to me, then she moves on to you. Next up, the mayor's office. Then, what the hell, why not the governor's?"

"You could be right," Donovan agreed. "But only about the chain of command, not about her motive."

"You know that, do you? She confided that to you inside her cabin last night?"

Donovan lost the easy attitude and pinned the sneering deputy with a level look as he stood. "What have you done to locate her cousin, Orry?"

"I'm here, aren't I?"

"Isabella said they drove through town in tandem. Have you talked to anyone who might have seen them?"

"She's yanking our chains, Donovan. There's no cousin."

"Have you been inside the manor?"

"What? No." The deputy controlled an obvious spurt of fear. "Why would I do that? Anyway, I don't have a key, and I'm not about to break and enter the place."

Donovan's gaze swept the unsettled horizon. "Manor's right behind us. I've got a key and permission to enter. You can come along, run back to town, or try and sell me on the fact that your kid's a genius and you have to buy him a new chemistry set. Choice is yours."

Orry opened his mouth to respond, but the sound that exploded across the ridge came from Darkwood Manor, not from him, as three bullets ricocheted off the rocks at their feet.

Spinning into a crouch, Donovan whipped the gun from his waistband, searched for the source. He spotted a rifle and an outline in one of the upstairs windows and fired. Then he lowered his arms and watched as both outline and rifle tumbled over the open sash to the ground below.

ISABELLA WAS INSERTING her key in the front door lock when she heard the shots come from the rear of the manor.

She'd seen a dilapidated garage back there and the remains of a stable, maybe an old icehouse. Someone could be using one of those structures for shelter. A poacher, perhaps?

"Well, that makes me feel better," she said aloud.

Crossing to the edge of the porch, she tapped her key on the worn siding while she considered her options. Only three came to mind. She could investigate alone, call Donovan, or get the hell out of here and let the acting sheriff handle it.

Okay, scratch the third thing. And who knew where Donovan might be. Halfway back to New York, where Haden said he lived, if he was smart.

Because, in the end, Mystic Harbor was all about ghosts. That and a recurring sense of being watched…

For a moment, Isabella let the creepy sensation slide through her. Did it come from the house, she wondered, or from some other source?

The fresh chill that skated along her spine had her hitching a shoulder and wishing she could ditch everything about this place. Except for Donovan. He was far too hot to ditch, and besides, he believed her about Katie.

When her cousin's face appeared, Isabella locked her gaze on the courtyard gate. Bolstering her resolve with the assertion that she didn't believe a word of the stories she'd heard last night, she drew a deep breath and made her way down the sagging steps.

Leaden clouds pressed in on her as she moved. Branches groaned, and whippy gusts of wind kicked up around her legs. An invisible crow began to caw, and more than once, wet leaves formed a whirling funnel in her path.

There were no more shots to be heard, and yet the feeling of being watched persisted.

Haden believed that evil had seeped into the very fabric of the house. Of course that wasn't possible, but for the moment she was alone, the skin on her neck was prickling—and why hadn't she called Donovan before coming here?

Logic warred with apprehension as she tugged on the gate.

Squaring up, Isabella sent the now-circling crow a level look and let a purposeful stride carry her across the cracked cobbles of the courtyard.

She fought her way through a second gate, this one made

of spiked iron, and finally reached the portion of the manor closest to the cliff.

The only visible path led her through an overgrown garden, down a tippy set of stairs and under a rotting pergola thick with vines and creepers. Thorns plucked at her coat and hair, but she persevered and eventually broke free of the cloying vegetation to a patch of ground covered in dormant roses.

She scanned the weedy beds. No unusual sounds reached her. Sickly bushes guarded the area ahead. Far above, she spotted a large, open window, and directly below it, something black.

Her first thought—snake—stopped her in her tracks. Her grateful second was that it looked more clothlike than serpentine.

Katie had been wearing a khaki trench with a black sweater under it. Palms damp, Isabella moved forward. She was nudging a prickly bramble aside when the ground cover behind her rustled and a pair of hands seized her arms.

"It's me," Donovan said before the scream in her throat emerged. "Did you hear the shots?"

With her heart attempting to jackhammer a hole in her chest, the best Isabella could manage was a nod.

"You do know you should have gotten back in your car and run, right?"

"Yes, I thought about that a split second before you grabbed me."

Donovan drew her into a crouch and pushed the dead roses aside.

With a fist pressed to her breastbone, Isabella stared. "What is that?"

He twitched a limp, black sleeve, currently snagged on a thorn. "I'd say it's an old suit."

"With no one in it." Her eyes rose. "What's an empty suit doing in this flower bed?"

He shifted the sleeve again to reveal a metal barrel. "Covering a rifle at the moment." His eyes rose. "Someone propped it up in the third-floor window. Orry and I were out on the cliff. Three bullets hit the rocks beside us. I saw a rifle—presumably this one—and a silhouette and fired... into the silhouette's arm," he added when she turned to frown at him. A faint grin tugged on his lips as he scanned the area again. "You want to know what Orry was doing here, right?"

"Well, yeah. I'm also a little curious about where he is now."

"He said he was going to call the incident in."

"To who? He's the acting sheriff."

"He'll remember that at some point. In the meantime, I want to take a look at that third-floor room."

"Because empty suits don't fire rifles, and ghosts don't pop in and out of them on a whim?" She exhaled a portion of her tension. "Donovan, what's going on here? Why would someone shoot at you?"

He pulled her to her feet. "Let's save that question for another time, call this evidence and take it with us into town."

"I thought... We're going into town now?"

"Right after we go through that room."

"But..."

Cupping her nape, he forced her to meet his eyes. "Someone fired three bullets from the window above us, Isabella. You assume those bullets were meant for me. But I wasn't alone on that cliff."

"I swear I've stepped out of the real world and into Wonderland." Isabella dragged a moldy piece of planking away from the third-floor bedroom wall. Donovan had her searching for cracks that might turn out to be hidden doors. "Whoever set this up would have had plenty of time to stroll right back through the bedroom door. No need for a secret passageway."

"We're covering the possibilities, Isabella." Donovan leaned out the window, looked up. "Why did your boyfriend buy this house?"

"Ex-boyfriend, and I'm still working on that."

"Was he eccentric?"

"A little. He liked psychic fairs. So did Killer, which surprised me."

"And Killer is?"

"His legal partner, a prosecuting attorney so nicknamed for his ability to tear apart false testimony in court and reduce the witness to rubble. Killer and Katie have had a turbulent on-again off-again for the past two years. That's how I met David."

"Are they on or off at the moment?"

"Not sure. Off, I think. I should probably call him. More importantly, I should call Grandpa C or Aunt Mara, but...I don't know."

"Text message?" Donovan assumed.

She breathed out her frustration. "I don't think she sent it, but they might. Grandpa C is forever pushing Katie to break out of her shell and do something wild. He says complacency breeds resentment, and Katie'll regret her steady lifestyle down the road."

"But you disagree?"

"Katie likes routine. Steady works for her. It just doesn't work for Grandpa C."

"He sounds like a control freak."

"He can be, but Katie's no pushover. He was furious

that she took up smoking in college and that hasn't stopped her."

"How did your grandfather feel about your ex?"

"David? Oh, way too flighty. He likes Killer, though, which is probably why Katie won't commit." She indicated the area in front of the window. "Have you found anything there?"

Donovan used his BlackBerry to photograph the dusty sill and floor. "Someone heavier than a ghost's been walking around up here."

Because the sky outside had gone from gray to black, she used the flashlight she'd shoved in her coat pocket to peer behind a broken headboard.

Once again, nothing. Next up was the armoire.

Did snakes like closed spaces, she wondered, then opened the squeaking door. Thirty seconds and one giant spiderweb later, she was swiping sticky threads from her arms.

While Donovan went into the hall, Isabella checked out the remainder of the wall.

The far corner was blocked. Unable to search there, she leaned on the wall and shone her flashlight through a hole in the ceiling. "You know, Donovan, that suit we found smelled awfully musty. Maybe someone got it from a trunk up in the…"

She stopped speaking when the wall behind her suddenly gave way. Unbalanced and too startled to react, Isabella toppled backward into absolute darkness.

Dark, that is, except for the unblinking yellow eyes her flashlight beam caught as she fell.

TOO MANY KIDS STILL VENTURED into the manor on midnight dares for the footprints Donovan spotted to signify much of anything. But he took pictures anyway and followed the ones he could as far as possible along the corridor. Still scanning the floor, he retraced his steps to the bedroom. "Isabella?"

A muffled cry reached him, together with several thumps.

Eyes sweeping from side to side, he crossed to the armoire and opened it.

He didn't see anything. However, he knew the thuds he was hearing weren't his imagination.

He attempted to pinpoint the source, had his hand on the paneling when a section of it sprang open and Isabella shot out.

"My flashlight broke." She let him catch her, but dragged him five feet away before using the cracked base to gesture. "There's something in there." She fisted the front of his jacket. "I saw round yellow eyes, Donovan. Snakes have eyes like that. I'm not going back in."

He resisted the urge to haul her up against him, didn't want to know where it came from.

"You don't have to go in," he said. "Just stay here and calm down. Breathe."

"I hate snakes."

"I noticed."

He kept a hand on her arm while he pushed the panel open. His penlight revealed an empty room, maybe six by eight feet, with a rectangular hole at the far end.

He shone the light up and around, examined all the corners, then switched it off and let the door spring closed.

"It's just a room, Isabella. No snake," he said, and was glad to see the visual dagger she aimed at him. "Whatever was in there probably got out through the vent. I'd go with a cat myself."

"Right. You know what?" Tossing her broken flashlight aside, she made a double-handed motion. "I'm done with this place for now. I want to know who shot at you and Orry then threw an old suit and a rifle out the window. I also want your acting sheriff to make some attempt to locate my cousin."

Donovan rearranged a long strand of hair that had wrapped itself around her throat. "Still not quite buying that text message, huh?"

She breathed out. "Katie and I are double-related. Her mother and my mother are sisters, her father and my father are brothers. We grew up together. I know how she thinks, how she acts, how she reacts. She wouldn't have left in the first place, but if for some inexplicable reason she had, she'd have called me. She didn't, so she must be in trouble. It's as simple as that."

Nothing about any of this was simple in Donovan's opinion, but something sure as hell was going on at Darkwood Manor.

He only hoped the air of gloom that seemed to be enveloping the old house had its roots in the present and not in a virulent strain of madness from the past.

Mystic Harbor lived up to its name, even in full daylight. The shops and storefronts had a faded, old-world look to them. The mist that drifted along the streets supplemented the haunted atmosphere of the town. Upper windows were shuttered, long planters were filled with herbs, and Isabella counted strings of garlic hanging in no less than five doorways.

"I thought garlic warded off vampires," she remarked to Donovan beside her.

"A little extra protection never hurts." He braked between the sheriff's office and a shop whose hand-painted sign read The Root of Evil.

She recognized Donovan's cousin, Darlene, smoking a cigarette on a bench outside a quaint brick office.

"You're about to be ambushed." Donovan twirled the

truck keys on his index finger. "If you want to run, feel free. The cruiser's not here. Means Orry isn't either, and you won't get any help from the other deputies."

Humor stirred. "But you will?"

He tucked her hair behind her ear. "I've got federal credentials, and friends in the IRS. Or so they've been told."

She couldn't help laughing. "You're good, Donovan." Then she surprised herself by sliding a hand down the front of his jacket and yanking him across the gearshift for a kiss that, despite its brevity, seared the edges of her control. That it also tempted her to go a great deal deeper was the only hitch—and the primary reason why she dragged her mouth away and gave his jacket a shake.

"Damn." A sparkle brewed in her eyes. "Your kisses rock, Black." The sparkle deepened to a tease. "For a fed."

His own eyes glittered in response. Isabella didn't know where things might have gone if someone's knuckles rapping the hood of Donovan's truck hadn't diverted their attention.

"Take it inside, you two. Later." Darlene crushed her smoldering butt. "My boss wants to meet Mystic Harbor's newest homeowner."

Donovan's lips curved. "You might as well go. I'm surprised old Gordie's held off this long."

"What does old Gordie want?"

"He's the local Realtor."

"Is he as subtle as the nonlocal developer?"

"Think steamroller, Isabella." Reaching past her, he shoved the door open. "You'll handle him just fine."

Because there was no Orry to badger, and Donovan only wanted access to the police computer, Isabella let Darlene whisk her across the street, through a shaded glass door and into the aftermath of a hurricane.

Computers, some dating back twenty years, littered the

reception area. Snapshots of every house in town lined the brick walls. There were three overflowing cabinets, two desks buried in paper, a sputtering printer in the corner and enough bottled water to float a square rigger, a model of which sat on a lopsided shelf outside a glass-encased inner office.

Darlene navigated the mess with ease and beckoned for Isabella to follow. When she knocked, a loud belch emerged from inside.

"Man's a prince." She shoved the door open. "You've got company, Gordie. Might want to polish up your manners."

The man who swiveled his chair to greet Isabella did so with a smile so broad it dwarfed the rest of his features. The skin of his face and neck was badly wrinkled and his bald head shone in the dusky light. As he stood to extend an over-tanned hand, Isabella's first thought was basted turkey. Her second was that he looked like a tortoise minus its shell.

"I'm delighted to meet you, Ms. Ross." He waved Darlene out, then rounded the desk to sweep a stack of files from a leather chair. "Gordie Tallahassee's my name. Not real, of course, but bland doesn't sell real estate, does it?"

"I really wouldn't—"

"Of course you wouldn't. Just call me Gordie and choose your poison. My bar's the best in town."

"It's eleven in the morning, Mr.—Gordie."

"Not in Venice."

"Excuse me?"

He spread his fingers and, to her amazement, his smile. "You make me think of northern Italy." Plopping down on his desk, he rocked forward. "Tell me, do you have any Dark blood in your veins?"

Her humor kindled by the absurdity of the situation, Isabella let her eyes twinkle. "No, but I have a Dark house on my hands."

"And therein lies our common ground."

Not bad, she thought. She'd been here less than two minutes and already they were talking property.

"Let me guess. You want to buy Darkwood Manor, or more correctly, you know someone who does."

He regarded her through heavy-lidded eyes. "I won't deny there's interest in your property, possibly more than you know. Oddly enough, none of those interested parties—David Gimbel excepted—saw the previous owner's desire to sell coming. I hounded the old coot for years to no avail. It got so every time I phoned, he'd swear and cut me off. Last time I called, he told me to contact him after Christmas. That was back in June. Two weeks later, David M. Gimbel struts into town, pleased as punch, and announces to everyone in hearing range that he's the new owner of Darkwood Manor. You could have knocked me over with a feather, Ms. Ross, and that's a fact."

"It's Isabella, and I'm not surprised. About David, I mean. He was a master finagler."

Gordie's smile tightened around the edges. "Not sure I'd use that term myself, but in any case, you're the owner now, and you strike me as a woman with a savvy head on her shoulders."

When his phone rang, he lifted the receiver and dropped it back in the cradle. His eyes, Isabella noticed, never left hers.

A light chill feathered over her skin. Shaking it off, she met his now-steely stare with a challenging one of her own. "Gloves off then, Gordie. You want Darkwood Manor. Unfortunately, so does my family. I'd call that a stalemate."

"I'd call that business." With his teeth bared, he rubbed his thumb and fingers together. "Money's what it boils down to in the end." He waited a beat, before adding a canny, "I hear you have a missing cousin."

"Your grapevine's fast and accurate. Any rumors on it that would help me locate her?"

"Sadly, no. Aaron Dark's a rather unpredictable specter."

Was he serious? Narrowing her eyes, Isabella asked, "Do you have a deal in the works with Robert Drake?"

His smile chilled. "What I've got, my dear, are buyers. One ghost more or less doesn't mean squat to them, but then most never see the properties they purchase, so Aaron's a non factor in their world. In yours—and as someone who was born and raised in Mystic Harbor, I can say this—you've taken on a great deal more than you can handle."

She continued to watch his face, wouldn't let herself react to whatever it was that lurked beneath the surface. "If you think scare tactics will induce me to sell, Mr. Tallahassee, you're wrong."

A tic made the loose skin of his jaw jump. "I don't have to scare you, Isabella. Aaron can do that much more effectively than any human."

"You said the same thing to David, didn't you?" she returned softly.

"Yes, I did, and less than a week after we spoke, he drove off a cliff. It got me wondering." Rocking forward once again, Gordie let his voice drop. "Just how much of the corporeal world do you suppose can be affected by someone on the other side?"

Chapter Five

Isabella marched into the sheriff's private office, planted her palms on the desk and looked Donovan straight in the eye.

"I want to see the police report of David's accident."

Donovan's lips quirked as he returned his gaze to the computer monitor. "You've got your left hand on it. But I can save you the trouble. There's nothing conclusive inside."

"I was told there was no way to determine whether or not David's car had been tampered with."

"Isabella, it was barely possible to determine what kind of car he was driving."

"So no one knows if he was alive or dead before he went over that cliff."

"He was alive." Donovan looked up. "David was talking to Haden when he hit the guardrail. What?" he asked at her surprised stare. "You didn't know that?"

"I knew he was talking to someone while he was driving. I didn't get a name." She regarded the folder. "Can I look?"

"Be my guest."

She indicated the back of the monitor while she scanned the contents. "What are you doing?"

"Checking out the rifle we found."

"Anything interesting?"

"Yeah, it's old."

She stopped reading. "Old enough to have belonged to Aaron Dark?"

"There's an eighteen seventies' patent on the model. Aaron died in eighty-one."

She was endeavoring to make out the handwritten report when he came around the desk and eased it free.

"I phoned Gunnar Crookshank, Isabella. He was first on the scene and in charge of the investigation. I'll get his take on what happened. We can go from there."

Less than a foot away from him with no obstruction between them, it suddenly struck Isabella just how compact the sheriff's office was. And how strangely airless.

"You, uh…" She shoved her thoughts in order. "Did you find any incriminating footprints on the cliff or inside the manor this morning?"

With his eyes still on hers, Donovan reached back to close the computer file he'd been reading. "All I discovered is that Orry's afraid of the manor, but then I should have figured as much since he's still terrified of Haden."

Air notwithstanding, a laugh bubbled up. "You're joking, right? Haden's a teddy bear. Gordie Not-His-Real-Name Tallahassee is the man Lucas needs to watch out for. Or just plain watch."

"He wants Darkwood Manor, huh?"

"And anyone standing between him and his goal out of the picture."

The office became a great deal more claustrophobic when Donovan wrapped his fingers lightly around her throat and slid them downward.

At close range, Isabella noticed a rim of gold around his dark eyes. The spell only shattered a little when he murmured, "Do you have a will?"

She made a strangled sound. "Do I what?"

"You heard me."

"Yes, I did. Yes, I do, and before you ask, my shares in the family business go to Grandpa Corrigan and Aunt Mara."

"What about your personal assets?"

There went the spell. She told herself not to grind her teeth. "You're wrong, Donovan."

"They go to your cousin, don't they?"

"My parents live very well in Boston." She kept her tone even. "I don't have any brothers or sisters."

"I'm not accusing Katie, Isabella, I'm just—"

"Being a cop."

A trace of a smile crossed his lips. He continued to hold her with his eyes—until his hand slid under her hair to the back of her neck. "You still scare the crap out of me, lady."

Breathe, she ordered herself as her vision began to cloud. Then, in a moment of pure recklessness, gave up the fight, curled her fingers in his hair and fused her mouth to his.

ALTHOUGH SHE KNEW SHE shouldn't, the woman chain-smoked while she waited. Fog rolled in to blanket the harbor side of town. It swallowed up boats and businesses, houses and haunted mansions. It made her skin crawl.

From her current perch, she could see Darkwood Manor directly across from her on the ridge. Thick, gray mist skirted the foundation, slithered up the outer walls and spread through the tangled gardens to the headstone at her feet.

A wail, long, shrill and somehow mournful rode the heavy whorls. She sucked in smoke, paced in agitated lines and told herself this was the surest way out of a very deep rut. Her ticket to ride—whenever, wherever. For the rest of her life if she was prudent and didn't wind up like David Gimbel, a pile of ashes at the bottom of a deadly cliff.

She smoked two more cigarettes before she heard the approaching footsteps. Did she see a figure near the manor at the same time?

She squinted through smoke and fog, but couldn't make anything out.

"What are you doing?" the person behind her asked.

"Not sure." She craned her neck. "I thought I saw someone. He's gone now."

"He?"

She wanted to snap at the droll tone, but thought better of it. "Why are we here," she asked, "when we know Isabella's still in town?"

"Work your brain, kiddo. Balance the fear factor against her stubborn streak. We need to do more if we want her gone."

Nerves jittered. "How much more?"

"As much as it takes."

She caught a gleam of metal as a knife embedded itself, blade down, in the ground next to an unmarked gravestone, and for a moment, wished she could walk away from all of this.

IT SEEMED EVERYONE IN Mystic Harbor was curious about the new owner of Darkwood Manor. Word that Isabella was in town spread faster than the fog that threaded its way through the streets.

The manager of the fish market offered her a deal if she decided to turn Darkwood into a hotel. So did the local butcher and two of the bakeries. As they were leaving, a fortune-teller from the Mystic Tearoom rushed out to give her a free reading.

Danger waited for her at Darkwood Manor. A man with dark hair wished her harm. Whether human or ghost the woman wouldn't say, but she added that Isabella could take heart because Aaron Dark's wife was on her side. Then she pressed ringed fingers to Isabella's forehead, clucked her tongue and whispered that it was sad when innocent blood was spilled. Sometimes, the tree of life bore bitter fruit. There were many secrets yet to be revealed….

Okay, Isabella reflected, as the woman dissolved into the mist, that was weird, but no more so than the arthritic Brothers Grimm who performed weekly rituals to cleanse the town of the evil still being generated by Aaron Dark's malevolent spirit.

A discovery that both surprised and delighted her was that Haden owned and operated a restaurant behind the sheriff's office. It was called the Cave, had a welter of round, wooden tables crammed into a long, underground room and was filled to the rafters with Dark-related memorabilia.

"Don't order from page two of the menu," Donovan warned as they descended into a den of smoke, herbs and flickering black candles.

Moody strings and pipes poured through mounted speakers, while a wall-to-wall collection of people dug into their entrées. She recognized most of the dishes, but figured a full quarter of the patrons had ordered from page two.

Haden waved them to a table under a smudgy charcoal portrait.

"Meet Sybil Dark," he said gruffly and gestured for her to sit. "Got something to show you. Donovan'll get you a drink. Make it strong," he advised, then settled his bulky frame and shook out a chart the size of a road map. It would have hung over the edges like a cloth if he hadn't refolded it into a rectangle.

"This is the Dark family tree. See these limbs here?"

She nudged his broad palm from the center. "I do now."

"There's Aaron and Sybil, and off to the right, Aaron's

sister, Millicent. Aaron and Sybil had triplets. They were nothing but babies when all hell broke loose up at the manor. After Sybil left, Aaron shipped them off to his parents in Virginia and let them do the raising. Which was a good thing in the end since, as you know, old Aaron eventually went mad. You following me so far?"

"Triplets, grandparents, unfaithful wife, madness. Got it. It looks like one of the three died."

"The girl died giving birth. The boys have their own stories. What matters here is that George and Darlene follow the daughter's line. Me and Donovan come down through sister Millicent's. Going back up the tree, the two of us have a bit of Moldavian, what we now call Romanian, royalty in our blood."

"Courtesy of a certain bloodthirsty count?" Isabella teased.

"Courtesy of a Moldavian prince whose wimpy descendant lost power after the occupation of 1821." He flapped a hand. "But that's not the point, is it? What I'm trying to say is that unless Millicent went mad like her brother, Aaron— and some say she did—then Donovan's worries about what might be waiting for him down the road are unfounded. It's George and Darlene who should be worried, and having met them last night, you can see, they're not."

Okay, now she was lost. "Why are you telling me this, Haden? I don't believe in inherent madness. Donovan's the one you need to convince."

"Yes, but I can't, can I, or I would. I need you to do it for me." He raised his voice and half his body to shout. "Watch that tray, Claudia. New worker," he explained, then winced as the young woman overbalanced in the opposite direction. "Keep the family tree, Isabella. Manor's yours. You should know what and who you're dealing with up there. Use both hands," he ordered the new server, then stood and rushed after her.

Donovan neatly avoided the rattled woman in the middle of the busy room. He set a bottle of red wine and two glasses on the table, pulled out a chair across from Isabella and sat. "So. Anything I should know about?"

She spun the folded chart. "The Dark family tree, specifically your branch. Haden says you have princely ancestors, but given the country and the time frame, I suspect Gypsy offshoots."

"My former sister-in-law would probably agree. My brother had nomadic tendencies throughout their married life."

As expected, the wine he poured was full-bodied and strong. "I didn't get that far down the tree. What's your brother's name?"

"Quinn, and before you look, he's dead."

Her voice and expression softened. "I'm sorry, Donovan. What happened?"

"He decided to try BASE jumping without a parachute. Didn't work out for him."

"Drugs?"

"Forensics said no."

She stopped him from raising his glass. "That doesn't make him insane, or validate your theory in any way."

"It doesn't support your belief, either."

"There's absolutely no precedent," she began, but a swish of air and a snap of gum interrupted. "I'm leaving in fifteen," a server with long, red hair announced. "Do you want to order now, or wait and let our newbie Claudia do the honors?"

"We'll wait," Donovan said.

The server pushed her sleeve up to reveal a watch with a

braided yellow-and-white-gold band. "I can check back in ten. Otherwise, I hope you're not hungry."

Isabella set her glass down so quickly that wine sloshed over the sides. "Where did you get that watch?" She managed—barely—not to make a grab for it.

"Some guy." The woman put a protective hand over her wrist. "It's not hot."

"Can I see it?"

"Are you a cop?"

"She isn't." Donovan flipped out his ID. "But I am." He indicated the watch. "Easiest thing all around would be for you to let the lady look."

The server, whose name tag read Lindsay, hesitated, then stuck her arm out. "There. See? It's not much. Probably turn my wrist green by the end of the night."

"Can I see the back?"

"Still a cop," Donovan reminded when Lindsay hesitated again.

"I don't have to do this." She pouted but gave in, flicked the clasp open and tossed the watch down. "There's nothing special about—" She stopped, frowned. "What are those letters?"

Isabella's fingers remained steady as she read aloud the engraving on the back plate. "From JDC to KLR." She raised her eyes to Donovan's face. "From James Donal Corrigan to Katie Lynn Ross."

ORRY SLASHED A HAND THROUGH the air. "It doesn't prove a damn thing." He had to shout to be heard over Lindsay and his deputy, who'd mistakenly believed he was the only man in her life.

"It proves Katie was in Mystic Harbor," Donovan replied evenly.

"Did I say she wasn't?"

"Yeah, you did. This morning, on Dark Ridge. Before those three shots were fired."

Orry ground his teeth. "I explained that, Donovan. I had to respond to a call—a speeder on the Coast Road."

"And Deputy Dawg over there couldn't have handled that while you checked out a potentially deadly situation?"

Orry's ears and neck reddened. "You prioritize your way, and I'll do it mine. Could be I prevented another person from flying off Cemetery Point."

Perched on a cabinet at the back of the office, Isabella smiled. "That's very conscientious of you, Acting Sheriff Lucas. But Donovan and I stayed at the manor for over an hour after the shots were fired. You didn't come back."

"What, you think a shooter'd have hung around that long? If you didn't find anything, what was the point of me showing up an hour later? For all we know, some college kid got hold of his granddaddy's old hunting rifle and decided to play a Halloween trick." When Lindsay's voice rose to a squeal, he slapped his knee. "Stop badgering her, Lee. You and Lindsay have been dating. She had some fun with another guy for a night. You've done the same thing yourself. Why don't you both go home?"

Donovan leaned against the door, preventing anyone from exiting. "The watch, Orry."

"What? Oh, right." He gave the silvery face a poke. "Tell us where you got it, Lindsay, this time without the hysterics."

She shot Donovan a mutinous stare, Orry a sneer and Isabella a watery-eyed plea. "He was just a guy. I met him over at the Raven on Wharf. We danced, had a couple drinks, got a little, you know…"

"Friendly?" Donovan suggested.

"Woozy," she snapped, then slumped in her seat. "Maybe

he slipped something in my drink." She appealed again to Isabella. "I don't remember what happened next."

Donovan circled her chair. "But you do remember him giving you the watch."

"I guess so. It was right before we left. He wanted me to come to his truck with him, but I said no. That's when he pulled it out."

"And then?" Orry pressed.

When she folded her arms, Donovan set his hands on either side of her chair. "What did the man look like, Lindsay? Can you describe him?"

Her breath huffed out. "It was dark, and like I said, I was feeling woozy. Pretty sure he had a beard. Or maybe it was just a mustache. Anyway, his hair was dark and sort of scruffy."

"Did he give you a name?"

"Nuh-uh. He said he was doing an Aaron Dark, and he was only in town for supplies, but when he saw me going into the Raven, he just had to follow."

Although a vein in her temple jumped, Donovan thought it had more to do with her glaring boyfriend than his questions. He continued to study her as he asked Orry, "Do you have anyone who can do a composite?"

"For a watch? Are you kid—?"

"I can draw," Isabella told him.

"Am I in trouble?" Lindsay asked.

Her boyfriend snorted. Donovan bit back a smile. "Not if you cooperate."

She turned in her seat. "You won't press charges?"

"I don't care about the watch," Isabella said. "All I want to do is find my cousin."

Orry stood. "I need to use the washroom. I'll dig out the art supplies on my way back. Meantime, Donovan, why don't you flex your fed muscles and make those two stop squabbling." This as Lindsay and the deputy resumed their shouting match.

Hopping from the cabinet, Isabella strolled up to offer Donovan a serene smile. "When did you say the real sheriff gets back?"

He fought an urge to run his thumb over her lower lip. "On or around Halloween."

"I was afraid of that." She glanced over as the phone rang—and rang and rang. "The deputy appears to be embroiled. Looks like you're it, Black."

Donovan waited through two more rings before reaching down and picking up. "Sheriff's office." He hooked Isabella's arm when she started to leave. "Where? Okay, call Abel's Towing, and wait for us to get there."

Keeping his eyes on Isabella's, he ended the call.

"Why a towing company?" she asked with remarkable calm.

"There's a vehicle hung up on the rocks half a mile from Dark Ridge. As far as the deputy can tell, it's a red, two-door sports car. Like the one you said your cousin Katie drives."

Chapter Six

Suspended by its left rear axle, the car was virtually invisible from the road. When the fog parted, Isabella spied a wheel, part of a fender and a portion of the roof.

The deputy who'd discovered it had two floodlights aimed at the swaying vehicle, but most of the light bounced off the fog.

Orry insisted it hadn't been there earlier in the day, but then Isabella reasoned he had to say that given his excuse for leaving the manor.

None of the volunteer search and rescue workers wanted to rappel down the cliff in the slippery conditions, so Donovan strapped on the gear and did one of the jobs he'd been trained to do. At the top, Isabella paced and breathed and told herself not to assume the worst.

Fragments of memory spun through her head. Vacations with Katie, school dances, boys, men.

She winced at the last two things. She and Katie had been a tad competitive where male attention was concerned.

With a rude "Yo, blondie," Orry strode over and shoved his two-way into her hand. "Your fed boyfriend wants to chat. Press the top button and speak up. Equipment's twenty years old."

"Donovan?" Isabella returned to the edge. "Is there anyone inside?"

"A woman."

Her heart leaped into her throat. "Is she conscious? Can you get her out? Is it Katie?"

"I don't want to move her, she's unconscious, and I don't know. What does your cousin look like?"

Hadn't she showed him a picture? Isabella pushed the hair from her face. "She's twenty-eight, five-six, average weight. Her hair's chin length, dark and layered. She wears three earrings in each ear and—"

"Hang on." Donovan's crackling voice was barely audible above the approaching siren. "It isn't Katie."

The knots in her stomach went cold. "Are you sure?"

"This woman's in her thirties. She has blond hair, and she looks shorter than five-six to me. Car's a Mustang."

And Katie drove a Camaro. Isabella didn't know whether to be disappointed or relieved. Either way, she was concerned for the injured woman.

"Paramedics are here." She glanced at the flashing lights. "They're unloading a rescue stretcher."

Orry snapped his fingers for the radio. "This is why I chase speeders, Ms. Ross. Sorry it's not your cousin."

Isabella ignored his sarcastic tone and rubbed her arms to ward off the damp, October chill.

"Freaky night, isn't it?" For some reason, the acting sheriff glued himself to her side as the paramedics started down. "Did you see that guy in the rusted-out pickup? He went past us like a bullet."

"The fog must have a weird effect on your bullets. That pickup driver was going thirty, tops."

"Yeah? Maybe I should use you instead of a radar gun."

"Maybe you should trade your radar gun for a police special and do the job your temporarily elevated status requires you to do."

"I told you yesterday, your cousin's an adult and—"

"I'm not talking about Katie." Because that would be pointless at this juncture. "Shots were fired at the manor today. A flesh-and-blood person squeezed the trigger of a very old rifle, then tossed it and an even older suit out a third-floor window. You want to talk freaky, there you go. I'd think, since those shots came within inches of your feet, that you'd be a little curious about who did the shooting and why."

As she spoke, she pivoted toward the manor. Oddly enough, the old house continued to drift above the fog. "Donovan said you were standing at the edge of the cliff...." She trailed off to stare. "There's a light on in the house."

"Light!" Orry stepped backward. "It's—it must be the moon—playing tricks."

Isabella watched as one light winked off and another popped on. "The moon's obscured right now, acting sheriff."

"Kids, then. It's October. Halloween's coming. You have to expect—"

The wail that reached them started out low and rose to an echoing screech that set Isabella's nerves on edge and had Orry's mouth opening and closing like a codfish. Backing up even farther, he stabbed an accusing finger. "I don't—I'm not—it's kids making that sound. Damn hooligans!" A yelp escaped as he hit a wall behind him.

Under different circumstances, Isabella would have laughed. She settled for letting her lips twitch, then pressed them together and waited for him to turn and see.

"Donovan, you bas—" A second wail cut him short. Fists clenched, he spun away to regroup.

While the paramedics worked on the woman below, Donovan came up behind Isabella and contemplated the manor. The lights continued to fade and glow at random intervals. They went out completely when the wail ended.

In an effort to disguise the quaver in his voice, Orry cleared his throat. "This is more than Crookshank had to deal with. Why's the spook show expanding now that he's gone?" He fired a resentful look at Isabella. "The whole thing started when Gimbel bought Darkwood."

"Meaning what, that Aaron Dark's spirit didn't want him around?"

"Him or you."

She harnessed her rising temper. "Do you know how ridiculous you sound?"

Bolstered by the return to normalcy, Orry's upper lip curled. "All I know is that outsiders are a pain in the butt where that house is concerned. If someone from the other side wants the place vacant, I say go along with him. What's one old wreck to anyone in Mystic Harbor? You should pack up and leave, lady, and count yourself lucky you can."

"Unlike Katie."

Donovan gave her arm a light squeeze, nodded forward. "There's a shadow on the ridge."

Isabella watched the anger, and undoubtedly most of the color, drain from Orry's face. "This is total bull," he muttered. "You two play spot the ghost. I've got an emergency to deal with."

Isabella barely heard him as she trained her eyes on the cliff that jutted out behind the manor. With wisps of fog streaming upward from the water, it was difficult to separate rock from tree and tree from—

"That's a man," she exclaimed and tugged on Donovan's jacket. "Do you see him? He's standing by a three-tiered boulder."

"He was," Donovan agreed.

She drew back, stared in disbelief. "Where did he go? He was there, and now he's not."

Donovan's lips quirked. "Maybe there's something hungry in the fog."

"Some carnivorous thing that swallowed him whole?" She stopped the shiver that wanted to ripple through her. "Evil doesn't live in fog, Donovan, and people don't vanish in the blink of an eye."

"Your cousin did. We will search the area around the boulder. Tomorrow." He caught her arm before she could start off. "There's nothing more we can do here, and Haden's server's still at the station. You have a sketch to draw."

Isabella studied him for a long moment, took in his guarded eyes and shielded expression. She saw the potential Gypsy, but no hint of the madness that had infected his ancestor.

Until those incredible eyes began to gleam and he circled her to drop his mouth close and whisper.

"Don't get complacent, Isabella. Everyone he met perceived Aaron Dark to be a kind and benevolent man. Only Sybil knew better."

Isabella suspected that the chill shimmering through her system had more to do with the man behind her than any lingering sense of unease. She forced a serene tone. "Nice try, Black, but you're forgetting my illustrious uncle, the Park Avenue shrink. I've also got your family tree in my coat pocket, the one that says you descended from Aaron's sister's—" she frowned, glanced around his arm "—line."

A screech of approaching tires filled the air as headlights blinded her. For a moment, she was simply too stunned to react.

Whoever the driver was, he was heading straight for them. And he wasn't slowing down.

DONOVAN SLAMMED AN ANGRY palm on the Cave's polished bar top. "I swear to God, Darlene, you pull a stunt like that again, I'll tie you up and throw you off Dark Ridge."

"And in that single, rash action confirm every fear you've ever had." Plunking her chin on the heels of her fisted hands, she batted innocent eyelashes. "Haden told me to drive fast, so I did."

"Didn't tell you to knock Donovan and Isabella off the road, though, did I?" Haden retorted. He'd doused most of the restaurant's lights and was overturning chairs onto tables with a vengeance. "Got word that a red car had flown over the cliff, Donovan. My first thought was that Isabella has a red car. I forgot she came into town with you. Darlene and me were driving fast but controlled. Then I heard the wail coming from the manor, and I panicked. Told her to step on it."

"So you see?" She wiggled her fingers. "Not guilty."

"Uh-huh." Although he wanted a shot of whiskey quite badly, Donovan held off. "So, what's the story with your boss?"

She shrugged. "He wants the manor. It's no secret. Land's prime for development."

"Enter Robert Drake."

"Him and about five others."

"Yeah, but Drake's the only one in town," Haden called across the room.

"That we know of," Darlene called back.

"Has he heard old Aaron wailing?"

She rolled her eyes, appealed to Donovan, whose response was to circle the bar and snag a beer.

"How would I know what he's heard?" She gave the table-top a grumpy swat. "I know Drake wants that property more than he's letting on. My mother saw him on Ridge Road yesterday."

A shocked Haden stopped stacking chairs. "George was on Ridge Road?"

"Well, obviously if she saw Drake there. It's not off-limits, you know. I drive it all the time."

"And sometimes smoke things other than cigarettes while you're there." Donovan tipped the bottle for a long drink. "She said she saw Aaron walk through a closed gate up at Darkwood."

Under his beard, Haden blanched. "You saw old Aaron?"

Darlene shot Donovan a baleful look. "I never said it was Aaron."

"What, you think Isabella's dealing with multiple spirits?"

"I think Isabella should sell up and go home. Forget themed hotels and profit margins, just take what she can get and run."

"Put an *X* beside her cousin's name in the loss column and close the book on her whereabouts, huh?"

Darlene drummed annoyed fingers. "Orry thinks she's full of crap, Donovan. No one he's talked to saw a cousin. Maybe Isabella's making her up."

"Like you made up a gate-crashing ghost?"

"I saw a man at the gate. One second on the far side, the next on mine. Who he was and what he wanted—no idea. I get spooked, I vamoose. Like Isabella would have by now if you hadn't jumped in front of her. Man, you must be lonely these days, cousin. A bit of skirt, a pretty smile and you go all Lancelot on us."

There were things Donovan could have said, but it wasn't worth the effort. Besides, his BlackBerry was beeping. Meant he had an email.

Shutting Isabella's face out—not an easy feat—he took another drink, regarded the screen and narrowed his eyes at the message that appeared there.

ALTHOUGH SHE KNEW SHE shouldn't, Isabella pulled on a wool jacket, grabbed her camera and a hot coffee and traded her fire-warmed cabin for a rocky seat outside.

The fog had dispersed. Under a bright, nearly full moon, she saw more than Darkwood Manor on the ridge. The headstones crammed onto the plateau below were also visible. Or partly visible, she acknowledged. Night continued to creep through the shadows.

Not eager to hear that wail again, she plugged into her iPod and turned up Sheryl Crow.

Memories of Katie swamped her. Good ones and bad. Like the road trip they'd taken to Florida after their high school graduation.

She recalled the boy they'd fought over in Fort Lauderdale. Isabella thought he'd looked like a young Brad Pitt. Unfortunately, he'd kissed like—well, not like Donovan, that's for sure. Not even close, she reflected, sipping her coffee and running her gaze over the manor's brooding silhouette.

Donovan's face hovered in the darkness ahead. She touched a finger to her bottom lip and smiled. Would Katie have wanted him, too? The smile became a laugh. Did people need air to live?

Sheryl segued to Bon Jovi. Moving to the music, Isabella unpacked her camera and adjusted the setting. Then a hand touched her shoulder, and her heart catapulted into her throat.

Whipping her head around, she hissed out a breath. "God, George, I thought you were a prowler." Not true, but as far as she knew, rifle-toting spirits didn't wander around looking for people to accost. "What are you doing down here?"

"Everyone's in bed except Mr. Drake. That man keeps the strangest hours. Up all night, sleeps half the day. Do you mind?"

Isabella shifted her coffee, used her camera to indicate the manor. "Even at a distance, the place has a sinister air."

George settled in, unscrewed a thermos. "I've felt it all my life. I've never seen Aaron or Sybil, but then I'm practical by nature and probably not in tune with such things." Taking a deep drink, she shuddered out a breath. "A little brandy'll kill the cold, but only if it doesn't kill you first. My daddy used to make this stuff in the barn. Brandy, wine and terrible beer. The barn burned down last year with my father and brother inside. I got the lodge, but the recipes are gone. There's only a few barrels of their home brew left." She poured a small amount into the cap and held it out. "Keep it to a sip," she cautioned.

Isabella hesitated—she hated brandy—then sucked it up and did the polite thing. Although her eyes wanted to water, she managed not to cough.

"It's very good." If you liked liquid fire. "Have you lived in Mystic Harbor all your life?"

"Yup. But for a twist of fate, I'd have been long gone by now. I like the city. Unfortunately…" She took another drink, set the thermos aside. "So, tell me, what do you think of Donovan?"

"Actually, I haven't—"

"Oh, come on, honey." George batted her thigh. "I can read faces better than that. You think my daddy's brandy tasted like gasoline—which it does—and you want to jump Donovan."

Isabella grinned. "You should moonlight at the Mystic Tearoom. You're right—Donovan's extremely jumpable."

"Or so women like to think." George rummaged in the pocket of her brown plaid jacket. "The man's sexy, he's hot and he's about as easy to reach or read as an October moon."

"Because of his connection to Aaron Dark?"

"We all have our fears."

"Or phobias." Isabella took a close second look at the base of a nearby rock. "What's that brown twisty thing?"

"That twig?"

She peered closer. "Not a snake?"

George picked up and tossed a pebble into the heart of the shadow. "No movement. I'd say it's a twig." She held up a crumpled cigarette pack. "Do you mind?"

"No, go ahead, I'm used to it." With an uncertain look at the alleged twig, Isabella asked, "Why is Donovan convinced he's going to follow in Aaron Dark's footsteps?"

"Has he told you about his family?"

"Yes, but you know it doesn't work that way."

"You have a fear of snakes. Why can't he have a fear of insanity?"

"Mine's a phobia," Isabella reminded. "It's a different thing, connected to a childhood trauma. I find it hard to believe Donovan's ever had the urge to imprison anyone the way Aaron imprisoned his wife."

"Imprisoned her without anyone in town realizing she'd returned. Haden tells the tale better than I do, but the nutshell version is that when Sybil came or was brought back to Darkwood, she was pregnant."

"By her husband or her lover?"

"That would've been the question in Aaron's mind. All he could do was lock her up and wait until she had the child. Never got that far, of course. She did or said something that set him off. Rumor has it that after he killed Sybil and her unborn child, Aaron went even madder, until, finally, one night, he took his own life. Rigged up a rifle, tied a string around the trigger and gave it a yank. Got himself right in the throat. Local minister found him in the rose bed three days later, faceup and staring at the house."

The rose bed. Under the pearled moon. Isabella aimed

her camera at the distant manor. "Was he wearing a black suit?"

George chuckled. "Not sure anyone's ever asked that question. Could be he was. Anyway, how did we get here when we were talking about you wanting to jump Donovan?"

"Ah, well, my grandfather says I have a habit of wandering. Off topic and destination. I get sent to Dallas, I detour to New Orleans."

George made an envious sound. "I've always had a yen to live in New Orleans. Sadly, I never will."

"Why?"

She motioned with her cigarette. "I'm tied to the lodge. Literally. By the terms of my father's will, the land can't be sold or developed for fifty years after his death. Unless I live to be a very old woman, that'll put me well past the hundred-year mark before I'm free. And before you suggest I hire a manager and spend my winters in the South, the profit margin's too small for me to do anything more extravagant than take the odd weekend trip to Boston. No, honey, unlike you, I'm well and truly stuck."

What could she say? Not much, Isabella decided, so she changed the subject and talked about the local Oktoberfest, Haden's Cordon Bleu cooking and, most intriguingly, what had prompted Donovan to become a federal sharpshooter.

"He's always had amazing eyes." George laid back on one elbow. "Darlene's are good—I swear, she can shoot wings off a fly at thirty paces—but Donovan can do the same thing at five times the distance and then some. Just incredible eyes."

No argument there, Isabella thought. She drank the last of her coffee and took a few more night shots of the manor while George stubbed out her cigarette.

"So," she said, "is your sexy-eyed agent coming back here tonight, or am I rushing things a bit?"

"You're rushing things a lot." A glint of metal in the bushes halted Isabella as she hoisted her camera bag and slid from the rock. Freezing, she looked down. "Uh, George, do people do much hunting in these parts at night?"

"Not that I know of. Why?"

Still staring at the ground, Isabella endeavored to work her heart from her throat. "Well, because something just came flying out of the bushes."

"What thing?"

Half afraid to move, she pointed to a spot directly between the toes of her boots.

There, embedded in a patch of hard earth, was a very large, very lethal-looking knife.

Chapter Seven

Someone had thrown a knife into the ground at her feet. From a distance. In the dark. Yet all Isabella could think about for the rest of the night was the information Donovan had uncovered.

A check of Katie's phone records revealed that someone from Bangor had placed a ninety-second call to her cell phone at the same time Isabella had been talking to their aunt Mara.

Isabella knew she should be pleased, or at least relieved. But she wasn't. Seconds after the knife landed, George had snatched it up and held it like a javelin.

"Oh, honey, I'm sorry," she'd apologized when she'd realized her mistake. "Donovan's going to be so angry at me."

He had been; however, he'd bagged the knife anyway, sent George back to the lodge and accompanied Isabella to her cabin.

He insisted on spending the night on the sofa. Isabella was disappointed, but did she really expect him to try and seduce her?

Nudging her into the bedroom, he told her to get some sleep. She did, but only because she was too exhausted to think straight anymore.

"The call to your cousin came from a pay phone," he

revealed at eight the next morning, when, tired and tousled, she groped her way into the living room.

The smell of freshly brewed coffee hit her instantly. Grateful beyond words, she located the machine, then propped her elbows on the counter to pour and drink. "I don't suppose you found any clues... Are those blueberry muffins?"

"George brought them down at dawn. Guilty conscience."

"She reacted. I stopped being upset about that part of it."

"So I get to be the bad guy, huh?"

His lazy drawl surprised her, almost as much as the glitter in his dark eyes. Both reminded her she was wearing nothing but a white terry robe that didn't come anywhere near her knees.

With her heart and stomach jittering, she raised the steaming mug to her mouth. "No diversions, Black. Pay phone. Where, who and theories on why."

"Location's easy. It's in the lobby of your family's hotel."

"My—really?" She hadn't expected that. "Katie was going to Bangor to check out the Boxcar's books. Someone from the office could have called her. Didn't want it known, couldn't do it from his desk, didn't have a cell."

"There are people who don't have cells?"

"Speculating here, Donovan. You're the cop." One whose eyes kept running over her legs, creating more sexual tugs than she needed to feel right now. She opted to circle the island.

Leaning across the counter and still too close for comfort, he let his lips quirk. "Coward."

She matched his smile, met him halfway. "I wouldn't have taken you for a morning person in that way."

"Depends on the inducement." His eyes slid to the vee of her robe. "Some are more irresistible than others."

Despite the heat that sizzled through her, she lowered suspicious lashes. "I don't trust that tone."

"You shouldn't." And catching her chin, he brought her mouth onto his.

If she'd been hot before, she felt scorched now. And hungry. No, ravenous. Greedy to experience sensations she hadn't felt for years, if ever.

Donovan's tongue dipped and tasted, pushing at the boundaries of her control and his. She wanted to feel more, however, the island between them was a barrier she couldn't sweep aside.

He raised his head to stare half-lidded. "We shouldn't be doing this, Isabella."

She caught his lip between her teeth, then released him to smile. "I know. Mystery text message, call from Bangor…"

"Old rifle, old suit, kitchen knife."

"You know how to kill a moment, I'll give you that." She stroked a finger over his cheekbone. "Your loss, Agent Black, because after my first mug of coffee, I rock mornings. Speaking of…" Her eyes flicked to the window. "Isn't there a triple-decker rock we're supposed to check out today?"

"Right after you draw a picture. And I have a chat with George."

"Okay. Uh, why?"

"There's a nick in the blade of the knife that was thrown at you last night."

"Which is significant because…?"

Eyes glittering once again, Donovan dropped a kiss onto her mouth that sent pretty much every question spiraling from her head. Until he added, "It was Darlene who nicked it two Christmases ago. That knife came from the kitchen of George's lodge."

IT WASN'T CHIVALROUS or fair, but Donovan left Isabella to turn Lindsay's convoluted description of the man who'd given her Katie's watch into a sketch while he went into town in search of Robert Drake. The man was a developer, and he was staying at the lodge. George allowed her guests to access the kitchen anytime, day or night. And she kept her knives in a rack on the counter.

He thought he'd have to return to the lodge, but he spotted Drake on a narrow side street. With a quick left-to-right look, the man ducked into a shop called the Apothecary.

He was examining a shriveled-up root when Donovan opened the door.

In keeping with the mood of the town, the space was heavily shadowed. Only a few dusty beams of light made it through a pair of mullioned windows. The proprietor, surely as old as the eighteenth-century glass, snored on his stool in front of a hand-operated cash register. Vivaldi played softly in the background.

Returning the root to its jar, the developer executed a ninety-degree turn. "You're looking for me, I imagine."

Donovan closed the door with his foot. "Why would you imagine that?"

"I heard there was an incident last night outside Ms. Ross's cabin. I'm a stranger in town, and I'm looking to buy land. In a material world, a little coercion wouldn't go amiss. On track so far?"

"I'll let you know once we're past the practiced stuff." Hands in his jacket pockets, Donovan strolled closer. "How did you happen to hear about this—incident?"

"Same way I learned you're a federal agent. Milt, the

fisherman eats breakfast at the lodge. He was talking up a storm this morning. Given the speed of small-town grapevines, I figure the shop owner there is probably the only person who hasn't heard the tale."

Although Drake's smile was as slick as his hair, Donovan spotted a fine line of perspiration on his upper lip. Time to nail down the source. He rested a hip on the glass-fronted counter. "I understand your brother's into magic, Robert."

The veins in Drake's temples gave a quick pulse. "I wouldn't call it magic, exactly."

Donovan shrugged. "Special-effects work is just performance magic. It's a fair call. Your brother's done shows on Broadway and in three major theme parks."

The veins bulged farther. "Sorry, I'm missing the relevance here."

"I doubt that." Donovan pushed off. "But I'll enlighten you regardless. Twenty years ago, you and your brother had a bad mind-reading act that you worked up and down the East Coast. The clubs you played were third rate, but high rollers occasionally go slumming. You met one and finagled a job. You sold real estate, got lucky, decided to branch out. I won't go into details, but the truth is, you've pissed off more than one landowner with your acquisition methods. Granted, you've never been brought up on charges, but I'm guessing that has more to do with embarrassment than anything else. You do what it takes to get what you want."

Anger darkened Drake's eyes. "You're bordering on a libel suit, Black."

"I'm only repeating what the people I contacted told me."

Drake clung to his composure by a thread. "Did you break into my computer?"

"That would be illegal. I spoke to one of your former assistants. She was more than happy to give me names, dates and telephone numbers."

"I don't throw knives at women."

"No, you slip things into their drinks and take it from there." Donovan held the man's glare, but he was aware of the hand twitching at Drake's side. "I'm just here to buy tea."

"Is that why you were looking at a mandrake root when I came in?"

"Looking isn't purchasing."

"It isn't administering, either, is it, in, say, a pot of tea?" When Drake's long finger grew even twitchier, Donovan figured he'd made his point. He tossed the developer a small brown box. "Try chamomile," he suggested. "It'll help you sleep. George says you're a night owl."

"Is that of some concern to you?"

"No, but it'll be of great concern to you if anything happens to Isabella Ross."

"Are you threatening me, Agent Black?"

Donovan grinned. "It's not my job to threaten."

"No? What is it your job to do?"

"I shoot." A razor-sharp gleam appeared in his eyes. "And I make it a point not to miss."

BETWEEN ORRY'S WISECRACKS and the young server's indecisiveness, the subject of Isabella's sketch came out looking like an 1840s prospector—dark, shaggy hair, droopy mustache, stubbly chin and wild black eyes. The result begged the obvious question: What could have induced Lindsay to dance with, let alone take a gift from, such a creepy-looking man?

In the end, Isabella figured the server probably hadn't given them any kind of accurate picture.

After leaving the station, she tried Katie's cell and home phones. No response. Again.

Inside her car, with the sun attempting to poke through a bank of mutinous black clouds, she punched Killer's personal number but wound up staring at her phone in disbelief. Who went fishing with his buddies and didn't take his cell? Incommunicado was fine, even admirable, but emergencies happened.

Frustrated, she tossed her phone in her purse, started the car and headed for Darkwood Manor. Donovan was meeting her there at two o'clock, and it was almost that time now.

She sighed when Gordie Tallahassee darted out of his office to flag her down. Dressed in a gray jogging suit and headband, he gripped the door when she lowered her window.

"Someone threw a butcher's knife at you!" he declared, aghast.

"Actually, it was—"

"How on earth did he happen to miss?"

Absurd laughter tickled her throat. "I guess whoever threw it either had good aim and wanted to miss or bad aim and didn't get lucky. You're, uh, leaking, Gordie."

"What? Oh, my bottle." The top had opened, allowing water to dribble down the front of his sweats. His teeth gleamed in a feeble ray of sunlight. "I run to keep fit. I went up Ridge Road this morning, heard noises coming from the manor. Have you spent much time up there, Isabella?"

"Some. What kind of noises?"

"Thumps mostly. Slamming doors. Did you know old Aaron used to throw furniture around when he got angry? He'd crash through the hallways like a man possessed until he reached the attic. No one knows what happened next, because the whole place would go silent as a grave."

"All I've heard so far is a wail," Isabella said, then wished she hadn't, because his expression brightened.

"That would be Sybil's death cry. Aaron knocked her out, but she woke up and realized he was going to throw her from the cliff. The last sound she ever made was a long, mournful wail."

"A wail she's only recently begun to make again."

"Ever since David Gimbel, a non-Dark, purchased the manor."

"By that logic, Gordie, nothing would change if I sold the property. And what about the previous owner? He wasn't a Dark, was he?"

The Realtor scratched a wrinkled jowl. "Hard to say. He's from the area. It's possible he had a drop or two of Aaron's blood in his veins."

"That's a very convenient answer. Mine's still no."

His smile froze in place. "In that case, I wish you luck. I also hope you find your cousin. Have you searched the rocks at the bottom of Dark Ridge yet?"

Although her muscles constricted, Isabella kept her voice light. "Why would I do that? Katie was inside the house when she disappeared."

"Rumrunners, Isabella." He tapped the door before straightening. "Rocks lead to coves, tunnels from caves lead to manor." His eyes took on a shrewd gleam. "And, of course, vice versa. I'm glad that knife missed its mark. But then I expect old Aaron's a bit rusty after all these years. The man was amazing in his way. He could shoot an arrow at an acorn and hit it dead center. I can't imagine a knife would be much different. Still, if I were you, I'd watch my back. Whether human or ghost, whoever threw it's not likely to miss the target twice."

OKAY, THAT WAS A THREAT. Delivered in a melodramatic fashion, but a threat nonetheless.

Good, Isabella thought. Because now she was angry, and anger was better than fear.

She drove up Ridge Road with one eye on the clouds and the other on Darkwood Manor. No way could a structure be evil. Even if ghosts did exist—highly unlikely in her current opinion—how could they harm a corporeal being? True, Aaron's story would make bookings soar and Grandpa C a very happy man, but beyond that, it was down to theatrics.

She hoped.

The wind velocity increased the higher she drove. It dispersed some of the clouds and allowed the sun's rays to gild the changing leaves. Light falling in pools on the driveway improved her mood considerably.

Until she reached the front stoop and saw an arrow protruding from the door.

"Might as well have signed your name to it, Gordie." Marching up the stairs, she used a gloved hand to wrench the shaft free. She held on to it and her resolve as she stepped across the splintered threshold.

The Realtor had mentioned caves at the base of the cliff, ones that led to the house. Somebody could have been lurking in a hidden room, spotted Katie and decided to take her, use her disappearance and the story of Aaron Dark's madness to frighten the new owner into selling the manor.

But why send a text message in her cousin's name? To keep her from contacting her grandfather and thereby risk a full-blown investigation?

Careful not to step on anything suspect, Isabella made her way across the entry hall toward the angel with the empty eyes. Lifeless or not, she felt like they were watching her. It didn't matter where she walked, the sensation persisted.

Well, damn, she thought in exasperation. Now she was

unnerved again, so much so that all she wanted to do was get back outside. But she wasn't going anywhere until she searched the ballroom again.

Shoulders squared, she played her new flashlight over the walls.

The paper covering them was old and peeling. In some places, it hung in long, water-stained strips. The remaining plaster had turned yellow with age. Someone, probably a kid, had spray painted one of the large exposed sections. She spied the words *Death* and *Danger,* and below that, more letters, partly hidden by a plank.

She angled her beam upward, paused, then brought it slowly back. The letters *I-S-A* jumped out at her from one side of the board, and *L-L-A* from the other. Tearing the plank away, she saw her full name painted in a garish scrawl.

Her heart knocked against her ribs. Backing up, she scanned the room. "Okay, this is sick," she accused out loud. "Do you hear me? This is just sick. Whoever you are, you're not going to make me believe—"

The sound came from directly behind her. She moved, but knew she hadn't done it fast enough when fingers gripped her throat.

She started to gasp, but a square of cloth covered her mouth and nose. The gloved hand tightened on her windpipe.

Both arrow and flashlight slipped from her grasp as her fingers went limp, and the ravaged ballroom went dark.

"I NEED TO SEE THE HOUSE again." Haden braced his palms on Donovan's dash. "Up close and personal. B'sides, there's more Isabella should know, and I've been dragging my feet about telling her. Don't hit the chipmunk!"

Donovan swerved around it. "I saw Darlene going into the sheriff's office today."

"Really? Think maybe Gordie was burgled?"

"She went through the back door, Haden."

The big man scratched his chin. "Can't figure why she'd do that. She never could stand Orry, and the other deputies are too young, too old or too soft to pique her interest. You sure it was Darlene?"

"I'm sure."

Trying to sound casual, Haden asked, "Speaking of interest, how's yours for a certain blue-eyed blonde?"

Donovan shot him a level look and said nothing.

"I gave her the family tree, told her to study it."

"Because she doesn't have anything better to do right now but immerse herself in our past. Someone threw a knife at her, Haden. A slime bag wants to buy the manor, her cousin's missing and Orry doesn't give a rat's ass about any of it."

"Orry is a rat's ass. Rut!" he shouted.

"I see it."

Haden shuddered, peered out. "I can feel Aaron's aura from here. Look through the trees. The clouds are coming back."

They appeared to be massing over the old house. Any second now, Donovan expected to see lightning bolts shooting down at the roof.

A glance at the dashboard clock told him he was late meeting Isabella. A few minutes might not matter to her, but it did to him. Because of that, he wanted to turn his truck around and get the hell out of Mystic Harbor before he fell into something he couldn't contain.

As he rounded the final bend, Haden went rigid. "I swear, there's a heartbeat deep inside that place. It gets louder the closer we get to the gate. You sure Isabella wanted to meet you here?"

Donovan's lips curved. "Why did you come with me again?"

"Don't be smart. I had to know if I'd feel the same way now that the manor's changed hands." He squinted through the gate at the overgrown drive. "What's going on up there?"

Donovan saw it at the same time. A man wearing head-to-toe black was carrying Isabella toward a nondescript van. When he spotted the truck, he tossed her in the back, jumped in and slammed the door. Gravel shot from under his tires as he gunned the engine and took off.

"Hold on," Donovan ordered his white-knuckled uncle. "He's heading for the back road."

A heavy wind sweeping in from the ocean bowed the smaller trees around them. They were almost directly under the storm clouds now.

Rain began to pelt the truck, falling in big, fat drops. Within seconds the drops became a downpour. Donovan switched the wipers on high and worked his gun from the waistband of his jeans.

Haden gripped the dash hard enough to crack it. "You can't drive and shoot, Donovan. I don't care how good you are."

Donovan kept his eye on the van's weaving bumper. The vehicle came and went from view, but he thought he might be gaining on it.

The woods on either side of Ridge Road closed in around them. Leaves, twigs and bits of bark joined the rain on his windshield. He drew a mental map, then swore as he narrowly avoided a pothole.

Haden sent him a frantic look. "What're you doing?"

"Take the wheel."

"I can't steer from this side. We'll crash into a tree."

"We'll have a better chance of not crashing if you take the wheel."

Without waiting for a response, Donovan lowered his window, leaned out and took aim.

His first shot hit the left rear tire. The blowout caused the van to veer sideways, but didn't slow it.

"Bastard's crazy." He aimed again. "Haden, keep the damn truck straight."

His uncle's response was unintelligible, but he steadied the vehicle.

As the van fishtailed, Donovan set his teeth and squeezed the trigger. The right rear tire blew apart.

"He's going off the road!" Haden released the steering wheel to point. Donovan grabbed it and swung his four-by-four through a shallow ditch into the woods.

The van was still a good hundred yards ahead when it collided with the trunk of a large pine.

The front end crumpled. Steam shot from the damaged radiator.

Donovan glanced at the trees beside him and realized he'd gone as far in as he could. Even crippled, the van's smaller size had given its driver an edge.

"Stay here," he told Haden before taking off.

The driver's door was visible, the passenger's wasn't. The front end was tilted into a steep ravine.

Donovan half slid, half ran down a long incline. Wind and rain slapped at him. Bits of woodland debris blew in his face. If procuring Darkwood Manor was his goal, whoever had taken Isabella would need her alive. If not...

He locked down a bolt of panic before it could take hold and skidded down the last few feet of the embankment. With his gun pointed skyward he approached the back of the van.

He saw nothing and no one inside. Either Isabella's

abductor had gotten out, or he was waiting in ambush. The only option Donovan had was to move in carefully and be prepared to act.

He swung in the driver's door with the trigger half squeezed.

The lone movement came from the floor in the rear. He recognized Isabella's blond hair and working his way in deeper felt for a pulse in her neck. Strong and steady.

His initial rush of relief turned to icy rage. He smelled the trace chemical and scanned the seats in front of him. There was no one else here, no keys, no open door, no indication of the direction her abductor had taken.

"She all right?"

His uncle's distraught face appeared behind him.

"She's alive." Donovan swept the area immediately around the van, spotted something black through the trees. Pressing a kiss to Isabella's forehead, he reached for the back-up gun he kept strapped above his ankle, handed it to Haden, then shut his emotions down and let his instincts take over.

"Try and revive her," he said. "Then take her to the hospital clinic."

"Why would he kidnap her?" Clearly shaken, Haden patted Isabella's hand.

"I don't know." Donovan exited through the back door. Adrenaline surged in his system. He kept his eyes focused forward. "But I'm sure as hell going to find out."

Chapter Eight

"I didn't see his face, Donovan. I heard a sound and suddenly there he was."

A headache from the chloroform throbbed in Isabella's temples. She circled the table, pushing on the pain points while Haden baked to settle his nerves. Donovan, who'd straddled one of the kitchen chairs, checked his gun and looked quietly dangerous.

Why that should excite her, she couldn't say. Well, actually, she could, but now wasn't the time.

Rain and hail blew against the cottage walls. Haden donned his potholders to slide a mile-high apple pie from the oven. He pushed a raspberry-custard tart into her hands on his way to the cooling rack.

"Darkwood's riddled with secret passageways," he said. "Got the floor plan of the house around here somewhere. I've done the numbers, and I'm telling you they don't add up. Measured from the outside, there should be more than twelve thousand square feet, yet the inside total's under ten. Those two thousand–plus feet have to be somewhere. I say they're between the walls."

Donovan shoved a fresh clip into his gun. "What about the caves Gordie told Isabella about? Real or not?"

"Probably real." Haden shook a warning potholder at Isabella. "Raspberries are good for concussions."

"But he didn't hit—"

"Cures a chloroform hangover, too. Unless you'd rather go to the hospital like Donovan wanted."

Isabella bit into the still-warm tart, then broke off a piece of the crust. "The guy might have said something as I was going under, but I'm not sure about that, either. I was trying to fight him off and not breathe at the same time." The look on Donovan's face brought the first glimmer of humor since she'd woken up in his truck. "You're still kicking yourself that he got away, aren't you? The fact that he had a huge head start doesn't play into it for you, huh?"

"I should have had him."

She sighed. "Katie disappeared in a matter of seconds. Should I blame myself for that?" Rounding his chair, she bent over to whisper, "You're not Superman, Black."

"You got the van," Haden called from the pantry. "Won't that tell you something?"

"Not if he's smart."

Isabella was glad to see Donovan roll some of the tension from his shoulders. She fought an urge to bite his earlobe and deliberately put some distance between them.

Cloudy thoughts coupled with an über-hot man in a lethal mood weren't conducive to smart choices. True, sex with Donovan was bound to be spectacular, but priorities were priorities, after all. She went back to massaging her temples. She really needed to stop thinking about him.

"I wonder if it was Gordie who sprayed that warning on the wall?" she mused. "If he also shot an arrow into the door, it would have been stupid of him to tell me he'd gone running on Ridge Road."

Haden snorted. "Stupid or cunning."

When the phone rang, Donovan reached over to pick up. There was a long pause before he asked, "How bad?" He glanced at Haden. "Yeah, I'll tell him."

"Tell me what?" Haden set fisted hands on his hips. "Did my pastry chef quit?"

"Not as far as I know. The Mystic Inn had a kitchen fire."

"What? Was anyone hurt?"

"Only the equipment. They were fully booked for tonight."

"I know." The big man waved a potholder at Isabella. "It's bridge night… Don't say it," he warned his nephew.

"They need another venue."

"Cave's got its own group of regulars."

"You also have a dining room upstairs."

"What about staff?"

"I can help," Isabella offered. "I've worked tables before. I've also had venues snatched out from under me."

Donovan tucked his gun away as a disgruntled Haden took the handset into the pantry. "Consider yourself a temporary server, Isabella."

"Why do I sense disapproval?"

Standing, he started forward, his eyes steady on hers. "This isn't your typical bridge club. These people don't play cards after dinner, they hold séances, every Wednesday night through October."

"Huh. Can't say I've ever waited a séance before."

When he stopped less than a foot away, it took all her willpower not to grab his hair and yank his mouth onto hers. But she'd done that before, and given the strained atmosphere in the cottage, they might very well wind up making out in the middle of the kitchen floor. "Wonder how Haden would feel about that?" she murmured with an abstract smile.

Donovan's eyes sparkled. "He'd probably leave by the side door and let us go at it."

Either he could read minds or her expression was revealing way too much. Whatever the case, she didn't falter. "Your call, Black. Do we help your uncle, or have wild, abandoned sex on his kitchen floor?"

With a shadow falling over him from the side, she could no longer see his eyes. But she felt his breath on her lips as he lowered his head. "Better to go with the odds."

Unable to resist, she hooked her arms around his neck and moved her hips against him. "Meaning I'm safer at a séance than I would be with you?"

"That depends."

"On what?"

He touched his mouth to hers. "On whether or not Aaron decides to show."

DEEP IN THE BOWELS OF the manor, he listened to water drip as he prowled and seethed and plotted. Too many things had slipped out of his control. He could work around the smaller problems, but not the big one, not the one that had blindsided him.

He wiggled his fingers, felt his temper take hold. He'd had her today. He'd chosen the moment and caught her off guard. Then, wham, enter the wild card, and his perfect plan had been shot to hell.

Eyes closed, he lifted his face to the stones overhead and made a solemn vow. Like his ancestor before him, he would claw his way back to middle ground, rebalance and begin again.

Oh, Isabella might very well still die. She just wouldn't be doing it alone.

"YOU MIGHT HAVE MENTIONED that this bridge-the-gap-between-worlds club was made up of grandmothers who use Ouija boards and tarot cards and take turns writing human-interest columns for the local newspaper."

Donovan led the way into the manor's cellar. "I might

have. But then you wouldn't have wanted to go, and every grandmother there was delighted to meet you."

"Yes, I'm gaining quite a reputation as the object of Aaron Dark's wrath. Remind me again why that's a good thing?"

"Because the more people who recognize you, the more careful whoever's after you will need to be."

She considered arguing, but held off. It was getting late, and they'd already been delayed by several hours.

First thing that morning, Orry had called to say a Jane Doe matching Katie's description had been hospitalized last night in Slade's Head, a town halfway between Mystic Harbor and Bangor. The woman couldn't remember her name or where she'd been going when she'd been struck by a car on the highway leading into town.

It wasn't much, Isabella reflected, but what could she do? She had to know.

The drive inland had taken the better part of two hours, courtesy of a construction detour. Add in an overworked, sour-faced police chief who hated the FBI, and the complications multiplied. If Isabella hadn't managed to steal a look at the mystery woman through the hospital door, they might still be there.

Jane Doe did indeed have dark hair, but she also had a nose ring, a mole on her cheek and a long scar across her right forearm. Details, Isabella suspected, Orry Lucas had been well aware of when he'd phoned.

Back in Mystic Harbor, rain drizzled from a gunmetal-gray sky. Haden insisted that exploring the rock near the edge of Dark Ridge was too dangerous in a high wind, so the cellar had won by default.

Donovan switched on a battery lamp. As some of the deeper shadows dissipated, Isabella searched the earth and stone floor for a trapdoor. "Why did you become a fed rather than a chef like your uncle?"

"Not a fan of squirrel pie, I guess." He made a subtle head motion. "Try the back wall. It's closer to the water."

She forged a path through a sea of rotted crates and barrels. "Is shooting your only job?"

"No more than asking questions is yours."

She'd walked into that one, but conversation was her best weapon against fear, and ever since they'd arrived, she'd felt as if some sinister presence was hanging over her shoulder.

"Going to find a snake, I just know it," she predicted under her breath. "They love dark places."

"So does my mother on a bad day." Donovan handed her a second lamp. "You're better off with a snake."

"Clearly, you didn't find one in your bed when you were six years old and you'd just finished watching a movie about king cobras."

He regarded her from his crouch. "Someone did that to you?"

"Right before my parents took me on a vacation to the Everglades. I don't know who it was, but I'm sorry I mentioned it, because it's not a memory I like to revisit." Swinging her flashlight in an arc, she located another doorway. "This cellar has an endless supply of rooms, doesn't it?"

"Probably." Donovan braced a knee on the floor. "But we might not need to look in them."

Giving her hair a precautionary shake for spiders, Isabella started across the floor. "Please tell me you found something."

A ghastly creak of hinges provided the answer as Donovan pried open a trapdoor previously concealed beneath layers of decaying boards.

She aimed her flashlight at a cobwebbed ladder and let an apprehensive shiver slide through her. "Next stop, the Dark depths of hell."

SHE WASN'T FAR OFF. EVERYTHING about the passageway spoke of a subterranean horror show. In Donovan's opinion, no one had been in this particular area for decades, possibly much longer.

The smell of moldy wood and earth was strong, the darkness thick and unbroken. Water dribbled from a ceiling that topped out at six feet. He had to duck in several spots to avoid whacking his head on sagging crossbeams.

At the first fork, Isabella shone her flashlight in both directions. "Left goes down, right widens as it climbs."

"Looks like left wins."

It was only the beginning. A dozen turns later, they reached a convergence that branched off in five directions.

"We need a GPS," Isabella remarked, then looked down. "Why's the ground sucking at my boots?"

"We're close to sea level."

"Figured as much. And the tide comes in when?"

A faint smile tugged on his lips. "Good question."

Incredulous, she raised her light to his face. "You don't know?"

"We can outrun an incoming tide, Isabella, as long as we don't get lost."

"So, no worries then. We'll just wait until we're knee deep in water and hope that one of the million side tunnels we've spotted and or taken leads up rather than down and doesn't dead-end like more than half the ones we've chosen so far."

He kept his eyes and flashlight moving. "Not having fun yet, huh?"

"Let's say this wasn't at the top of my to-do list when I came to Mystic—what was that?" She whipped her beam around his arm.

"A scrape. I've heard it twice."

She hissed out a breath. "You know, Black, you could

be a little more alpha cop here, seeing as I'm a city girl with absolutely zero spelunking experience. There's another scrape."

He drew the gun from his waistband. "Walk in front of me."

She didn't argue, merely slipped around his arm and let him listen.

He detected one scuff of rock, then another. The second one ended with a squish.

"Hell." A telltale click had Donovan thrusting Isabella into a narrow passage.

The first shot hit stone and ricocheted. The second whizzed past his right arm.

"Stay here," he told her. "I'm going back."

"What? Why?" She grabbed his sleeve. "Donovan, that's crazy!"

Another bullet raced past. Pulling out a second gun, he pushed it into her hands. "Crazy's what I do." He dropped a quick kiss on her lips. "Stay low, stay quiet, stay here. Anything moves, shoot it."

"What if that anything is you?"

"It won't be," he promised and left it to her to fill in the blanks.

The ones involving the shooter's objective, Isabella's safety and his own dead body.

SHE GROUND HER TEETH to keep them from chattering. She'd give him thirty seconds, thirty-five tops, before she did something. No idea what, but damsel in distress wasn't an option.

She heard three more shots in rapid succession before the passages went eerily silent.

Water sloshed when she moved her foot. The tide was definitely coming in.

Several seconds ticked by. The silence held. *Time to move,* she thought, and turning her flashlight on briefly, stole a look around the damp corner.

Nothing scraped or squelched, and no more bullets flew past. Full darkness prevailed. The rustle of her jacket made a deafening racket. The ground water had crept up and over her boots.

Drawing a breath, she started to step out. A stealthy swish to her left halted her. Her heart pounded; her stomach became a mass of slippery knots. Was there someone close by, or had a chunk of earth fallen from a wall?

With her thumb on the flashlight switch, she considered her options. The feeling of being watched had grown to mammoth proportions. But how could anyone see through impenetrable darkness?

Obvious answer: no one could. She was letting fear choke reason. She should be more worried about Donovan's safety than her own. Why had the shooter stopped firing?

With her gun hand on the wall, she pointed her light straight down, hit the switch—and gasped when the beam revealed a pair of boots less than four feet in front of her. Big ones, black and unmoving.

She jumped back, snapped the light up, then for a shocked moment simply stared. Until the man's hands rose, and he took a step toward her.

Panic clawed through disbelief. She splashed back into the passageway. "Donovan!"

Stumbling on the uneven ground, she evaded the out-stretched hands. Gun, she remembered, and fired a warning shot into the high shadows.

"Donovan, there's a—!"

He knocked her with his shoulder, spun her face-first into the wall. Light bounced off the ancient beams. She didn't fall, but she lost her grip on the gun.

Strong hands on her arms wrenched her around. She rammed a fist into hard flesh, heard a whoosh of air.

"Dono—"

She broke off when the man tossed her roughly aside. As her knees hit the ground, he vanished into the darkness.

Terrified, Isabella grabbed the gun, regained her feet and ran in the opposite direction. She was approaching a Y-shaped fork when she slammed into another hard body.

Her knee came up in automatic defense. It would have connected if Donovan's voice hadn't said, "Isabella, it's me."

Her muscles didn't want to unlock, but she managed a shaky, "Thank God. I thought he'd circled back."

"Who?" He gave her a light shake. "Who circled back?"

"A man. He was in that passageway back there." Over-whelming relief gave way to sudden urgency. She snatched up the sides of his jacket. "Donovan, it was him. The man Lindsay described to Orry and me yesterday. The one who gave her Katie's watch!"

Questions about the mystery man's identity and his agenda zinged through Isabella's head. Unfortunately, the more imperative question was: Would she and Donovan escape from this hellhole before the tide rushed in and trapped them?

Wincing as icy water slopped over the sides of her boots, she shone her light along the passageway. "At the risk of sounding pessimistic, we're going downhill again."

Donovan angled his beam upward. "Trick of the eye."

"So the fact that the insides of my boots were dry a few minutes ago and now they're not is irrelevant?"

"Yeah."

She used frustration to block fear. "Is there some reason you're talking in monosyllables?"

"I'm thinking, Isabella."

"About what?"

"Take your pick. The guy who knocked you out yesterday, the one down here today, your cousin, her watch, the knife that was thrown at you, the arrow in the front door, the threat on the wall upstairs, Gordie Tallahassee, Robert Drake…"

"Orry Lucas's wild-goose chase."

"That was just him being a jackass. He got stuck in Mystic Harbor when his aspiration was to be like your ex. Free and loaded."

"Someone should tell him about the grass being greener. David was loaded all right, but I wouldn't have called him free. He had a lot of responsibilities, most of them work related, and an equal number of personal demons. He was a quirky man, and the fact that his stepfamily was deceptively nasty made him a moody man as well. Which is probably why I own Darkwood Manor and they don't."

Donovan steered her to the left. "Gimbel was prone to moods?"

"Could be. It's not necessarily a bad quality."

"Is your cousin moody, too?"

A fist tightened in Isabella's chest. "Katie's a rock. Killer's her only vice, and he's not as radical as his nickname sounds. David was a different matter. She said he reminded her of her father. Manipulative, self-centered, greedy."

"All those negative qualities and you still got involved with the guy?"

"Well, I didn't know at first, did I? Besides, David wasn't anywhere near as manipulative as Katie's dad. She's jaded where certain types of men are concerned. She'd like you, though." A smile blossomed. "She's a sucker for sexy eyes. The water's up to my knees now, Donovan."

"I know."

"Any idea where we are?"

"Yeah." Draping an arm over her shoulders, he lowered his mouth to her ear and whispered, "We're lost."

Chapter Nine

He wasn't joking. The water was hip deep by the time they found an actual uphill tunnel. Fifteen minutes of difficult slogging ended at a narrow set of stairs that led into an old outhouse.

Isabella regarded the bench-style toilet with a doubtful eye. "Very weird place for a tunnel entrance."

"Location answers one question, though." Donovan opened the outer door. "The stone ledges over there form a natural stairway up to the ridge."

Tugging off a boot, she dumped the water out. When she saw where he was looking, she hopped closer. "That's the three-tier rock, isn't it? Six big steps above a tunnel entrance. Our shadow from the other night had an escape route." She noticed that Donovan's eyes were directed toward town. "Something else?"

"Lindsay met the man you saw today at the Raven. It's possible someone else met him and knows something."

After pulling her boot back on, Isabella regarded the ratty ends of her hair. "Is there a dress code at this club?"

"Yeah, leather and felt."

"Excuse me?"

Setting his hands on her waist, he boosted her onto the first ledge. "It's Oktoberfest."

THE DATES MIGHT BE A little off, but the atmosphere in the harborside club was nothing short of boisterous. And yes, there were people dressed in leather pants and Bavarian hats.

An oompah rock band played German music on stage while the crowd danced and drank and stuffed bratwurst sausages in their mouths.

Finally, something that didn't relate to Aaron Dark. Isabella welcomed the break. Showered and rejuvenated in jeans, high boots and a black turtleneck, she dropped her coat onto a long bench.

"Place has charm," she acknowledged. "Is that a portrait of Aaron Dark next to the bar?"

"Aaron Leisberg Dark," a man behind her corrected. "One must acknowledge both parents." Looking absurd in short pants and thick, white socks, Gordie Tallahassee plucked two glasses of beer from a tray and offered them to her and Donovan. "On the house." He thumped his chest. "Mein house."

Isabella tried not to laugh. "You own this place?"

"Part of it. My brother who lives in New York has the lion's share."

And he didn't like that one bit. She gestured with her glass. "What were you saying about Aaron Dark's parents?"

"Sit." He pressed her onto the bench. "Donovan can mingle while I tell you the tragic tale of Aaron's mother. I warn you though, it's a rather gruesome story."

She thought it might be glee that lit his leathery face as he plunked himself down and clinked his glass to hers.

"A toast, to Aaron Leisberg Dark, a madman through no fault of his own. The fact is, my dear, Aaron's mother tried to kill him a few short weeks after he was born."

DONOVAN KNEW THE STORY well. He also knew that Isabella would be perfectly safe while he walked around. There was nothing Gordie loved more than to frighten people with his version of the local lore.

His mind slipped backward as he moved through the crowd. He'd screwed up big-time down in the tunnels. Somehow, the shooter had gotten past him. He'd tracked the five shots deep into the system. The farther he'd gone, the less passageways he'd encountered. The footsteps he'd heard had been well ahead of him before they, like the bullets, had stopped.

He'd considered going on but had decided to backtrack and find Isabella. Less than halfway there, she'd shouted his name, and everything inside him had turned liquid.

The bastard shooter had gotten around him.

Sipping his beer, he controlled the emotions swirling darkly in his belly and searched for the disconnect that would allow him to think the way he should. Or not, he reflected when someone's fingers crawled slowly up his back.

"Aren't you the sweetie-pie, letting Gordie the Gorgon highjack your lady thirty seconds after you arrive." A smirking Darlene leaned into him. "Pretty city girl starting to get to you, cuz? But how do you protect someone you're starting to care about from a ghost, and a vicious one at that? Best way I can think of would be to make her leave."

He caught the finger she'd started to drill into his ribs. "I had a more practical solution in mind. Bust the ass of whoever's trying to run her out of town."

"Ooh, now you're going all John Wayne on us."

"Yeah? Who's us?"

She tugged on her hand. "Everyone. Me, my mother, Gordie, the waitress over there who's ogling your butt…"

"Orry?"

Increasingly vexed, Darlene used her other hand to pry

free. "How should I know? When did you get so literal anyway?"

"A couple hours ago, after a bullet flew past me in a tunnel under Darkwood Manor."

She stopped moving to stare. "Someone shot at you? I know you're a fed and all, but—well, why?"

"No idea—yet."

"That sounds…" Her brow furrowing, she gave her slinky top a tug. "Wait a minute, did you just say there are tunnels under the manor?"

"I said tunnel, not tunnels."

"Oh, crap. Here we go again." She jabbed the air in front of him. "I don't know what your deal is, Donovan, but I haven't done anything, so lay off the bait."

"You want it straight, tell me who's trying to bully Isabella into leaving Mystic Harbor."

"How do you equate someone shooting at you with an attempt to bully her?"

"We were in that tunnel together." He took a drink of beer, scanned the growing crowd. "Someone wants Isabella gone. That same person probably wanted Gimbel gone as well."

"Are you saying this mystery person tampered with his car?"

"Could be."

She slashed an X through the air. "Man, I do not need this tonight. I came here for a good time, and I intend to have one."

"Well, hell, honey, you always do that." George's slurred voice came from Donovan's left. She used her hands like grapple hooks on his shoulder. "Going outside for a smoke break, Agent Black. Wanna join me? I warn you, though, I'm in a major funk. I applied myself to the lodge's books today and discovered I'm seven K in the red for September.

Tack on another four from August and two from July, and I'll be well on my way to bankruptcy by spring. While that might make Daddy's nasty old proviso go away, it could also land me in one of Gunnar's cells, because where else am I gonna go with no money, no credit, no job and no roof?"

"Don't sweat it, Ma." Darlene glowered at Donovan. "You can get a job at Darkwood Manor when Isabella's family turns it into a hotel. Of course it'll take a bit of money to make the place habitable, and one titanic exorcism to get rid of the resident ghost, but barring disaster they'll need someone on the front desk." She paused to let a satisfied smile slide across her lips. "I hate to be the bearer of bad news, cousin, but your pretty bird's ditched her perch."

Following her gaze, Donovan saw a bench packed with people, but no Isabella.

And even more disturbing, no Gordie Tallahassee.

"STOP GLARING AT ME." Isabella strode ahead of Donovan down a black-lit corridor. "I don't need your permission to use the washroom."

He caught her by the arm, swung her gently around. "I'm sorry, Isabella. I saw that you and Gordie were gone, and I overreacted."

She regarded him for a moment, then decided he was sincere. "Okay, apology accepted."

"Simple as that?"

She scratched at the zipper of his jacket. "I don't hold grudges, Black, contrary to Grandpa C's insistence that any self-respecting grandchild of his should." She brought her mouth to within an inch of his bottom lip. "As for leaving me with that sadist who calls himself a Realtor..." The kiss she gave him would have cost her her focus if she hadn't kept a picture of Gordie's turtlelike face firmly in place. "Do it again, and I'll shoot you." She nipped the corner of his mouth. "With your own gun." She rolled her hips into his. "In more than one vulnerable spot." Drawing back, she let her eyes glitter. "Savvy?"

"Maybe." Catching her waist this time, he hauled her against him. "But just so we're clear…"

Nothing about Donovan's kiss was playful. There was no sense of discovery, no lazy exploration. No tasting, no tempting, no going slow. Tonight, with everything that had happened and so much upheaval inside, it was suddenly all about heat and hunger and unrestrained desire.

His mouth took possession of hers in a way that made her want to possess right back. His tongue plunged in deep while his fingers under her hair held her in place.

Not that she wanted to go anywhere. What she wanted to do, what she very nearly did, was let her own fingers tear his shirt apart so she could run her hands over the muscles of his chest.

Instead, she fed off him and walked that fine line between reason and desire. She could pull away now, or give in and allow the heat inside to billow and surge until it consumed her.

She couldn't help flirting with temptation. Donovan was dark and dangerous and completely intoxicating. His kisses were a drug to her system. There was something wonderfully forbidden about the way his mouth ravaged hers. The taste of him slapped back any thought of resistance.

He'd gone rock-hard against her. She wanted to take him in her hands. Not feel him through his jeans, but go skin to skin, with no words, no barriers and no reason to stop.

Tiny points of heat pricked her skin as his mouth left hers to run along the side of her neck. When his hand moved to her breast, her head fell back. It amazed her how much pleasure such a simple touch could evoke.

Damn, he was good at this, too good under the circumstances. But she didn't want to think about that. Didn't want to care. Might not have if a cluster of cowbells jangling nearby hadn't yanked her back.

She felt Donovan's lips curve. "Ten-second slam." He pressed a kiss to the vulnerable spot under her ear, then raised his head a fraction. "Down your drink in less than ten seconds, and the next one's on the house."

With a sigh of regret, Isabella loosened her grip on his hair and dropped her hands to his shoulders. "Ten seconds more, and drinks wouldn't have been the only things going down." She summoned a hazy smile, rested her back on the wall. "We need some separation, Donovan. I do anyway."

The cowbells clanged again, a raucous sound that shouldn't have made her laugh but did. She supposed she should be grateful for it even if she didn't appreciate the intrusion.

When Donovan skimmed a kiss across her still-warm lips, she let her smile widen. "That better not be another apology, Black."

He ran his thumb along her lower lip. "You're playing with ancestral fire, Isabella. You don't know what I might be capable of. Did Gordie tell you about Aaron Dark's mother?"

"Yes, and in today's world, we have two words for her medical condition. Postpartum depression."

Before Donovan could respond, a door banged opened and George rushed in, smelling of smoke and beer. "There's a guy in the parking lot, slashing tires."

With his eyes on Isabella's, Donovan asked, "Where's Orry?"

"Probably passed out under a table. It's his night off, and that was the third round of cowbells in the past hour. It's a big knife, Donovan."

He reached behind him for his gun. "Go into the main

room with George, Isabella. If you see Orry, tell him to get his butt outside." Catching her chin for a quick kiss, he warned, "Don't follow me."

More people ran in. "It's Denny Lucas," one of them shouted.

"It was probably him the other night, too." George shooed Isabella along. "Rumor is he carried a switchblade in high school. Come on, hon. There were a lot of people on the side patio, and getting stuck in this little corridor won't be much fun if they stampede."

A second wave of partygoers bolted past. An elbow sank into Isabella's ribs. "Is this the only entrance from the patio?" she asked.

"It's the easiest way in. Don't know why Denny goes ballistic from time to time, and it's a sure bet Orry won't get any answers from him. But in the end, I suppose we all have our triggers."

Isabella ducked as someone holding a fire extinguisher high in the air ran against the flow. "This is insane. What's Denny's trigger? Too much liquor?"

"Can be, but it's early for that. I'm thinking Darlene. They were a couple once upon a time. Denny never could let go."

"And slashing tires makes him feel better?" A heavy foot landed on her toe. "Ouch. George, stop pushing. I can only move as fast as the people in front of me." And there were at least a dozen, all shouting for someone, anyone, to stop the crazy man outside before he punched a hole in their tires.

For the life of her Isabella didn't know where it came from, but when she glanced down, there was a paper napkin in her hand.

A chill skated along her spine. She stopped moving forward, and after a slight hesitation, stepped to the side.

"What are you doing?" a bewildered George demanded.

Nerves quivered in Isabella's stomach. *Don't look,* her brain whispered. But her hands ignored the warning and opened the napkin.

The words, written as if by a child, leaped off the surface.

STAY OUT OF MY HOUSE!

ISABELLA DIDN'T KNOW what disturbed her more, the note that had appeared out of nowhere or the sight of Denny Lucas up close.

The man was big, bald and terrifying to behold. His shirt and pants strained at the seams, and he was missing three fingertips on his left hand. He scowled as he tore and lit matches one by one from a ratty pack. To her surprise, he shot more lethal looks in Orry's direction than Donovan's.

"I got a little crazy." He regarded a burning match. "Only stuck ten tires."

"The ones on my brand-new truck being four of them," Orry accused.

"Five." Denny extinguished the flame with a surprisingly light breath. "Got your spare, too."

While Orry turned three shades of red, Donovan hoisted himself onto a cabinet. "Why'd you do it, Den?"

"Wouldn't you if you had the chance? Come on, Donovan—Sheriff left a weasel in charge of things. Say different, Orry, and I'll do your station wagon next. Charge me, and I'll rip out your lily-yellow liver."

"I'm not going to charge you," Orry said through his teeth. "But I expect to be compensated for my loss."

"What about the other vehicles?" Donovan asked.

"I got the first mixed up with Orry's. I only did one tire on the third. That was just me being riled up."

"No one paid you to create a diversion?"

"Hell, no." He struck another match, let it singe his thumb and finger. "I do for myself, not others."

Donovan's tone remained pleasant. "I heard you lost your job at the processing plant last month."

"Me and thirty other guys. Cutting tires isn't gonna get it back."

"Just made you feel better, huh?"

"Yup."

"In that case—" Donovan hopped down "—we're done."

Finally, Orry spluttered back to life. "What do you mean, you're done? You hauled him in here."

"I did you a favor, Acting Sheriff. The rest is up to you. By the way, you've got lipstick on your collar."

Denny snickered and tore off another match. Orry's cheeks lost their color. It boiled back up a moment later, along with the veins in his neck. "Get out of here, the pair of you. You've been a pain in my butt since we were kids, Donovan, and your girlfriend there is either looking to drum up publicity for her ill-gotten gain or she's working on some kind of delusion. I still haven't seen any sign of a cousin."

With the napkin tucked deep in her pocket, Isabella raised unperturbed brows. "Does that mean you've been to Darkwood Manor and conducted a thorough investigation?"

"I don't have to investigate. Damn place is a deathtrap. It should be condemned. No one with half a brain would set foot through the front door."

"Means he's still afraid to go inside," Donovan said.

Denny snorted out a laugh. "Got bigger fish to fry's more like it, because he's sure as hell's gone in. I saw him do it a couple days ago. I downed three beers and chopped a couple bushels of firewood before he slunk back out. Now, what do you suppose a weasel would be doing in a haunted house for more than an hour?"

Orry's lips thinned to near nonexistence. "That's it. All

of you, out. Now. Before I toss you in a cell and throw away the key."

In spite of everything—and the day had been jam-packed—a laugh climbed into Isabella's throat. She'd never seen anyone go from red to white to green in the space of five short minutes. Until now.

"Come on," Donovan said while Denny glared his cousin down. "I want to see that napkin again."

Isabella didn't, but she drew it from her pocket when they reached the sidewalk. She frowned. "Do you think Denny really saw his cousin at the manor?"

"Probably." Donovan held the napkin up to the streetlight. "This is written in lipstick."

"Maybe it's Sybil who wants me gone." She tipped her head for a better look. "It's not the same color as the lipstick on Orry's collar. That was Bordeaux. This is poppy red. Guess his wife's not the culprit."

"She's not." Donovan continued to study the note. "Orry's wife doesn't wear lipstick."

IF ISABELLA HAD BEEN tired before, she was exhausted by the time she staggered into her cabin. Donovan wanted to work on his laptop, and yes, he told her flatly, he planned to camp out on her sofa again.

Fight it or let it be? she wondered wearily. Going into the bedroom, she stretched her arms up to release the tension.

A lavender-scented bubble bath should have improved her mood, but her emotions continued to fluctuate with every twist and turn of thought. By the time she'd drained the tub and wrapped herself in a white bath towel, she was more sick of the ups and downs than the strain of the day itself.

A soft nightlight came on when she extinguished the overhead light. She considered opening the door, but that would only lead to trouble. She wasn't coy enough to play the kinds of games David had accused her of playing before their breakup. Dinner with a coworker was business, whatever he might have believed, whereas contact of any sort with Donovan was a sexual minefield waiting to explode.

"Okay, stop," she said out loud. "This pissy day ends here."

Determined, she drew the shade halfway down. She thought she spotted movement in her peripheral vision, but when she looked, there was nothing. After folding the quilt back, she shot a last smoldering look at the door, and started to drop her towel.

It might have been a faint rustle of fabric that alerted her, or maybe some innate sixth sense. Whatever the case, her hand and eyes froze when she noticed a bulge under the sheet.

The hot fear that leaped into her throat threatened to choke her. She wanted to scream, but shock prevented any sound from emerging.

She was six years old again and too terrified to move. She could only watch in numb horror as a long, mottled snake slithered out from under the sheet and turned its slitted eyes toward her.

Chapter Ten

No one who worked at the Boxcar Hotel in Bangor would admit to placing a call from a phone in the lobby, even when the police came through.

Seated on the floor, with his back propped against the sofa, Donovan drank black coffee and went over what little he had.

He'd sent a sample of the suit fabric to Portland for testing. Fiber analysis put the manufacturing date between 1925 and 1930, long after Aaron Dark's time.

Three bullets had been fired from the rifle they'd found in the rose bed, and that weapon had been in production back then. However, the lipstick used to write tonight's napkin message likely had not.

As for the van Isabella's abductor had abandoned in the woods, the vehicle had been stolen from a used-car lot two towns south of Mystic Harbor. The thief had left no traceable clues behind.

So far they had a sketch of a man who could be placed both at the Raven and in the tunnels under Darkwood Manor. They had a dead ex-boyfriend whose car hadn't been tampered with, a missing cousin, a knife that had landed mere inches from Isabella's feet, and in Donovan's case alone, a tension headache that was endeavoring to hammer its way through his skull.

He felt restless and irritable, and despite the fact that he'd heard water running thirty minutes ago, he wasn't going to find an excuse to go into Isabella's room.

Like a lifeline thrown to a drowning man, his computer signaled a late-night email from Haden.

Going into Darkwood Manor tomorrow. Maybe. No ghost's gonna say I can't. I'll be there at 5 p.m.— maybe—if you or Isabella happen to be in the neighborhood. Bringing the floor plans. I want to see the writing on the wall and the entrance to the underground passageways. I repeat, want to see. Not sure if I have the backbone to actually do it. Haden.

The last few lines had a smile grazing Donovan's lips. Even so, he knew where his mind would be spending the rest of the night, and it sure as hell wasn't on the sofa.

Seriously out of sorts now, he drained his mug, thought about going for a walk. Maybe a blast of cold night air would beat the lust into submission.

He was reaching for his jacket when he heard Isabella scream. Grabbing his gun instead, he ran for her door.

His first thought was that someone had come in through the window and taken her. He refused to acknowledge the second.

Kicking the door open, he swung in gun first.

"No, don't," she said and pointed with an unsteady finger. "I'm fine. But—right there."

He saw the snake at once and lowered his arms.

"Don't say it." She sidestepped toward him. "Just make it go away, and we'll be good."

Donovan held a hand out to her. "It's not moving, you can get past."

"What kind is it?"

"I don't know." He did, but why make things worse? "It's only watching you, Isabella."

"They always do."

She said it through her teeth and barely loud enough for him to hear. But she looked pissed off, and he preferred that to terrified.

Closing the gap between them, Donovan tried to block her sight line. She'd turned off the overhead light, and he hadn't thought to turn it on when he'd come in, so he went with a table lamp that only partially illuminated the bed.

Her fingernails bit into his ribs. "Why is it staring at me and not you?"

"Must be a boy snake." He tucked his gun away. "There's a blanket on the chair by the door, Isabella."

"I see it. I'll get it."

Because the door and chair were close together, Donovan left her to it while he walked to the foot of the bed.

The snake was loosely coiled, flicking its tongue and, he had to admit, staring at Isabella. Smart boy snake.

"It's a rattlesnake, isn't it?"

He smiled. "If you knew that, why did you ask me earlier?"

"Making conversation, Black. It helps combat hysteria. Blanket."

He caught it, then hearing the warning rattle from the bed, made a head motion. "You don't have to stay. I'm not going to hurt it, and it's not going to hurt you. There's coffee in the kitchen, and my coat's on the hook by the front door."

On the way out, he handed her his second gun and told her to lock the door behind him.

Ten minutes and a short hike into the woods later, he returned to the cabin. She wasn't wearing his coat, anymore, but the towel had given way to jeans and a blue T-shirt that made her eyes look like misted lake water and his groin go hard.

She was in the kitchen and more composed than he'd expected. Her forearms rested on the island counter, and she had two bottles of wine in front of her.

"I found these in the cupboard." She blew at a layer of dust. "They're homemade, probably crappy, but at this point I'd settle for George's daddy's high-octane brandy."

"She still got that?"

"Supply's running low, like her finances, but yes. Why did he put a proviso in his will against a sale of the lodge?"

"Because he was a bastard." Donovan started toward her. "Don't you want to know what I did with the snake?"

"Far away from me is all I care about. What I would like to know is who put it there."

So would he, but not now. He kept moving, told himself to back off. Unfortunately, his body had stopped listening to his brain, and God knew, his common sense had deserted him a long time ago where Isabella was concerned.

She touched the corks with her index finger, one, two, then touched the tip of her tongue to her teeth. "Wanna choose?"

"Not especially."

"Thought not." A sparkle swam up into her eyes. "I can't guess what's on your mind, Agent Black."

"Then you must be a lot less perceptive than you look."

Pushing off from the counter, she strolled across the shadowed floor. How the hell could jeans and a T-shirt get him harder than a skimpy towel? He'd been out of the dating loop too long, and out of his mind since he'd met her.

She kept coming, even after he halted, until she was close enough to hook a finger in the front of his shirt.

A smile played on her lips. "I love a man with a conscience. Just not one so massive it gets in the way."

"You know what I want, Isabella."

"Good, so no games then." Releasing his shirt, she wrapped her arms around his neck and, jumping onto his hips, fused her mouth to his.

The last thought that formed before Donovan's hormones took over was that he hoped any madness lurking inside would kill him before it killed her.

ISABELLA DIDN'T CARE if she died right then or not. At least she'd go out on a sexual high like nothing she'd experienced before.

Her grandfather's finest whiskey paled next to the taste of Donovan's mouth. She felt hot and tingly and eager for more.

Secure on his hips, she allowed herself to explore. Greed and need collided as his tongue slid over her teeth. The hands on her bottom rolled her against him. Desire whipped up with so much force she thought sparks might literally start to fly.

Breathless and quite frankly shocked, she dragged her mouth free. "I think I'm drowning."

"Do you want to stop?"

She tugged on his lower lip. "Not stop, only pause. I need to breathe for a minute before I submerge again. I'm not used to feeling like this."

"Hot and bothered?"

"Oh, I left that one in the dust before you kissed me." Moving to his ear, she nipped the lobe. "I'll settle for over-come and warn you that I plan for us to go on a truly spec-tacular mystery tour tonight. Just not in the bed, okay?"

"Not a problem," he murmured and captured her mouth again.

With his kiss sending her airborne, Isabella could almost believe she was riding on a cloud. All the night sounds merged. The cool cabin air only made the fire inside her that much more intense.

Something solid bumped against her back. She worked feverishly at the buttons of his shirt, then gave up and tore it apart. When he brought her away from the wall, she dropped her feet to the floor and attacked the snap of his jeans.

In some distant corner of her mind, she realized that Donovan was far more adept than her. He got her top off between kisses and had his mouth on her breast before her fingers reached his fly.

A gasp escaped as he circled her nipple with his tongue. Every nerve in her body jolted. Sensation streaked from breast to thigh. With the wall behind her once again, she let her head arch and her fingers go still. But only until she felt the strength of his erection.

A sense of urgency took over as every thought in her head funneled down to a single basic need. She wanted him now, this minute, while her muscles could still function and her brain could still respond.

She wondered vaguely how much heat a person could take before she became a mass of sizzling nerve ends, one melting into another. Did it matter?

"I should hate you," she managed at length. "I never give anyone this much control."

"Makes two of us." His tongue explored the valley between her breasts, before beginning a lazy ascent to her throat. "If you want to stop, tell me now, Isabella, because in about five seconds, there'll be no going back."

"Scary thought, isn't it?" Her fingers danced over his skin. "But I'm thinking it's time I faced one of my bigger fears." Snagging the ends of his hair, she hauled his mouth back onto hers.

It seemed like a race to her overheated mind, a mad dash toward a line she couldn't see, because everything around her had gone black. There was only sensation left and the understanding that whatever happened beyond this point could be as dangerous as the threats on her life.

Should she run from that, she wondered, or go with it and see where it led?

If an answer existed, it got tangled up in need as the last of her clothes disappeared and the cabin began to list.

Heat streamed like lava through her veins.

Sweeping her into his arms, Donovan took her to the sofa, then followed her down with his own body.

She wanted to see him, but there wasn't enough light, and her hands couldn't be everywhere at once.

"We're going too fast," he said against her lips. "We need to slow down. I need to—" When she bit him, he stared for a moment, then shook his head. "To hell with it."

Her mouth curved into a vaguely feline smile that became a sudden gasp when he slid his hand between her thighs and began to stroke her.

A new fire burst to life inside. Her head bowed on the cushion, and a cry came from deep in her throat. Dark heat flowed through every part of her. She raised her hips to meet him, and only remembered to breathe when he left her to alter the angle of their bodies.

Color bled to shadow and shadow to sparkling black. Within those tiny snaps of light she glimpsed his face, his eyes, possibly his fears.

But they were fleeting images, there and gone in a heartbeat. It was the storm of emotions inside that drove her. She wanted to ride them, cling to them, savor and not release them until the last one slipped from her grasp.

The night dissolved to a blur. The scent of Donovan's skin and hair made her crazy. She wanted to feed on his energy, then spin it around and give it back.

When his mouth closed on her breast again, a moan of

pure pleasure escaped. Her entire body thrummed. She ran her hands over his ribs to his hips, then inward until her fingers closed around him.

He had protection. She didn't know how it appeared or where it came from, only that it was there.

Maybe slow was better, maybe it left more of a lasting impression, but right then all Isabella could think about was the flashover, that heat-bursting-into-flames moment when there was no thought, only a full sensory burn.

He could do that to her, she knew he could because— well, because he was doing it.

The drumbeat in her head was echoed in every one of her pulse points. His hair tickled her cheek. He said something she couldn't hear, then linked his fingers with hers. Bringing her arms over her head, he raised himself above her and slid inside.

Isabella's breath caught and held, so tightly that her head began to swim. Then there it was—the moment. The glorious climax that shot shimmering threads of light through the dark. Wicked licks of fire erupted inside as she bucked her hips to meet him, thrust for thrust, in a rhythm so strong it very nearly had her seeing stars.

Energy whipped around her. She saw his eyes gleam and, freeing her hands, gripped his shoulders like a lifeline.

Again and again, he pumped himself into her, until the spiraling light threatened to suck her into her own orgasm.

Control. She'd held fast to it in the past, and without much effort. But not tonight, not with Donovan. For the first time in her life, she'd given herself completely to someone else.

While the wonder of that was likely to linger for a very long time, she recognized the sliver of fear that danced on the edge of her brain. Ignoring it was child's play for the moment, but would it be as easy in the full light of day?

Because she wanted nothing to intrude on the after-shocks still shivering through her, she glided her foot over his leg.

"You know, you're heavier than you look."

"Dead weight always is." But he shifted to his side and, as much as he could, kept her from tumbling to the floor.

"Don't see this working for long." Catching his shoulders, she laughed. "This puts a whole new spin on the phrase 'living on the edge.' Maybe we should build a fire and... whoa!"

He caught her before she hit the floor.

"That's it." She held on with both hands. "We need to take this down before we start thinking too much about the shoulds and shouldn'ts of the past hour. Not that I'll be able to think for at least another hour, but being a federal agent, I figure you're trained to snap back faster than the rest of us."

A smile hovered on his lips. "Do you always talk this much after sex?"

"Only when my teeth are chattering."

"You think a fire'll change that, huh?"

Safely tucked in now, she ran a finger over his cheek. "Unless you can think of something better."

"Not really."

She sighed. "You're not going to go all monosyllabic on me, are you?"

"I might." Holding her gaze, he slid his hand between her legs.

"Damn!" Her hips rose automatically to meet him. "That wasn't fair, Black."

"Life seldom is."

Her response was to wriggle free, straddle him and trap his hips between her knees. With her palms pressed to his shoulders, she bent forward until her lips brushed over his. "Okay, my turn. I'm going to show you how a former Girl Scout can take a spark like that and turn it into an inferno."

THE WOMAN ARRIVED AT their rendezvous point ten minutes late—and didn't like the self-satisfied expression on her partner's face.

"What have you done?" she demanded. "Did you hurt her?"

He held a knife up to the weak overhead light. "I doubt it. Isabella strikes me as someone who can move pretty fast."

"What does that mean?" She glared at him, arms folded, until he lowered the blade.

"Your faith in me is staggering."

"And your plan is starting to suck. What did you do?"

"I played on a weakness *you* told me about and put a snake in her bed."

She tapped a cigarette out with agitated fingers. "Was it a constrictor?"

"You're such a girl. A rattler's far more affective."

"You bastard. I warned you—"

He moved as fast as the reptile he'd sicked on Isabella, jumping to his feet and whipping the knife up. "You were saying?"

With the tip of the blade pressed against the underside of her chin, she was half afraid to swallow. But she held his gaze, took a drag from her cigarette and angled the smoke toward the ceiling. "Jerk her around, and you jerk him even harder. Screw up once, and he'll be all over you."

"What, you think that scares me?"

"He's a fed, a sharpshooter. He hit that suit I propped up dead center before I could blink. Do you really want to mess with that?"

He scraped the blade across her skin, glowered for a

minute, then backed off and tossed the knife aside. "The goal hasn't changed, only the numbers. We're dealing with two now instead of one." An ugly grin split his face. "Looks like we'll have to be a little more inventive. And a whole lot more mean."

Chapter Eleven

Consequences, repercussions and second thoughts…

Every word was a lash on Donovan's conscience. The damage was done. All he could do now was make sure any blood spilled belonged to him.

"You're as stubborn as ten mules," Haden accused. "Maybe twenty." He waved a whisk at the fridge. "Get me some milk and eggs, then sit down and drink your coffee while I finish this French toast for Isabella. No arguments—you're taking it to her if I have to follow you back to the cabin. You mad yet?"

Donovan shot him a look as he reached for the milk. "Getting there."

"Good, now hit me."

"What?"

Haden stuck his bushy chin out. "Take a swing, hard as you can. Don't matter where. Jaw, stomach, lower if you're feeling as cranky as you look."

"Haden, I'm not—"

His uncle stepped forward. "You want me to go first?"

"No, I—"

"Fine, I will." And drawing back a big ham fist, he went for the head.

Swearing, Donovan ducked, caught his uncle's wrist and

swung him around with his arm locked firmly behind him. "Have you lost your mind?"

"Could be," Haden growled. "I'm a Dark, aren't I? Just like you and your ma and George and Darlene, too. We've all got the blood, so it follows we're all genetic time bombs, ticking toward insanity." He jerked his trapped arm. "Am I making my point here?"

"Yeah. You're ready to join my mother in Bellevue."

"Make that thirty mules," Haden muttered. "Aw, hell, let go of me before your breakfast burns."

Releasing him, Donovan picked up his coffee and aimed a venomous look at his uncle's back.

"I felt that, Donovan. Funny thing, though, I got you smoking mad, and yet here I am with all four limbs still working. Do I hear thunder?"

"Maybe. It's raining. Are we done with the drama for now?"

"You promise to take this breakfast to Isabella?"

"Dammit, Haden, yes, I'll take it to her. You know it's possible she has her own reservations about last night."

"You mean because of that shyster ex of hers?"

Irritated but calm, Donovan poured more coffee. "Did you like the guy on any level?"

"About as much as I like that bloodsucker who's staying at George's lodge."

"Drake."

"D'you know he's already bought a hundred acres of land north of the manor? Heard he's haggling for two hundred more to the south." Haden gestured with his spatula. "You mark my words, he's gonna make a move on Isabella at some point. I can't figure out why he didn't jump on her the minute she came to town, but I figure he's got some strategy going. Any ideas what all the moaning and groaning we've been hearing is all about?"

"One or two. Nothing concrete."

"What about Isabella's missing cousin?"

"Same answer, less definite."

Haden slid the French toast into a hot-pack, sealed the lid and popped a bottle of syrup on top. "Go, eat, talk. Think family tree. Remember, it's George and Darlene who're direct descendents of old Aaron. No one ever proved his sister was crazy."

No one had ever disproved it, either, Donovan thought, jogging through the wind and rain to his truck. He had to plant that thought firmly in his mind and not let the memory of a night spent with Isabella sway him.

Yes, he cared. More than he should or had for any other woman. All the more reason not to take a chance on the future state of his mental health.

Flipping his jacket collar up, he regarded the mist-shrouded manor. That look didn't falter when a low, keening wail joined briefly with the wind, rose to a mournful crescendo, then faded to eerie silence.

He might believe in the possibility of genetic insanity, but he sure as hell wasn't buying into any ghost.

It was past time for the manor to reveal its deep, dark secrets.

ISABELLA EMERGED FROM the bathroom to the sound of someone's fist hammering on the door.

A voice called from the other side. "Honey, it's George. I've got a message for you."

She started across the room barefoot, in her robe, towel-drying her hair.

No surprise, Donovan hadn't been here when she'd woken up on the floor under layers of blankets in front of the still-glowing hearth. She'd expected him to be gone by first light.

Truthfully, she'd expected him to leave before that, but she supposed she'd given him good reason to stay.

"Honey? I see your car out here. Are you home?"

Isabella spied a hot-pack on the island with a note that read:

Hope you like French toast. Haden sent enough to feed everyone at the lodge. Working on your cousin's disappearance. Don't imagine there's any point telling you to stay put. Donovan.

"It was great for me, too, Black," she said with a grin. Still toweling her hair, she continued on to the door.

"Isabella…? Oh, good, you are there." George lowered her hand. "I saw the lights on, and you always turn them off when you leave."

Isabella drew her inside, glanced at the ominous black clouds and shook off—she wasn't sure what. Possibly one of those feelings that struck when certain elements seemed a little off. Like the way George was dressed, in a pale blue dress with a white vest and bright red pumps.

"Well, hey there, Dorothy. Where's Toto?"

George regarded her shoes. "They were on sale. I click my heels together every time I put them on, but so far, no Oz."

"The shoes don't take you to Oz, George, they take you home. Coffee?"

"No, thanks. I have an appointment with a loan officer at the bank which I'm not looking forward to. I stopped off because I have a message for you from Donovan. He's somewhere up on Dark Ridge—possibly broken down, I didn't quite get that part—and he wants you to meet him at the manor."

"Really?"

"You sound surprised."

"I am. Last time we arranged to meet, things—well, never mind. Did he say when?"

"ASAP was my understanding." Clasping her hands, George glanced into the wall mirror. "Wish me luck today. I'm going to need it."

"Should I say break a leg, or is that only for..." The smile on Isabella's lips faded. "You're wearing lipstick."

"It matches the shoes. Is it too much?"

"No, it's nice. Would you, uh, call the color poppy red?"

"I guess so. Look, hon, if you want some, just go on in to the drugstore on Vermont. They're giving out free samples this week."

"To everyone?"

"To all their female customers." She waved a hand in front of Isabella's face. "Are you feeling okay?"

"What? Yes." Isabella recovered quickly. "Meet Donovan at Darkwood Manor." And go to the drugstore before it closes. "Thanks for the message. Good luck at the bank."

She drummed her fingers on the door after George left. Lipstick warning on a napkin; free drugstore samples in town. Someone wanted her gone. She could come up with a few names that worked, but what about Katie? How did her disappearance fit into this?

Determined, she started for the bedroom, pausing only long enough to snag a piece of Haden's French toast. Her cell phone beeped while she was cramming a big bite into her mouth.

Swallowing with difficulty, she regarded the screen, then slowly pressed the message button.

Sorry, Bella. Big mess here. See you soon to explain. Don't call Killer. Katie.

THE CLOUDS WERE LOWER, thicker and somehow more forbidding up on Dark Ridge. Isabella suspected her mind was embellishing the atmosphere, but not by much.

Rain, driven by a punishing north wind, slanted down in sheets. The thunder that rolled in the distance was punctuated by flickering bolts of lightning. And lurking beneath it in her mind, a second text message from Katie.

There was no sign of Donovan or his vehicle, but the door to the manor was ajar, so she dropped her keys in the pocket of her long coat. Given the state of the windows and the webwork of underground tunnels, the lock was a token in any case.

The air in the great hall felt damp and oppressive. Plaster crunched under her boots. Wind whistled through gaps in the walls.

Talk about setting a mood.

She managed not to jump when her cell phone rang, however, her heart refused to leave her throat, and that surprised her.

She picked up. "Isabella Ross…Grandpa, hello. How are you?"

That was all the opening her grandfather needed. There were a number of *I wants* and *you shoulds* before the dreaded question arose.

"Katie's not here," she hedged. "I haven't seen her since Monday. What? Really? You got one, too? No, it isn't like her." She suffered the usual lecture until her brain simply got tired of listening. "I'll call Killer again tonight. It's possible she's with him. Yes, I know, he can be secretive. I'm going into the cellar. No signal there. I'll be in touch as soon as possible. Love you. 'Bye."

Slapping her phone closed, she turned it off and slipped it into her pocket with her keys—and the Black family tree, she realized when her fingers brushed the folded paper.

It reminded her that Donovan was a Dark, with either Romanian royal or more likely Gypsy blood mixed in. Whatever the combination, he knew how to make love.

Now, why would her mind go there? Not that a hot man she might very well be falling in love with wasn't preferable to the creaks and groans of a crumbling cliffside mansion, but she'd been assaulted here before and could be again if she wasn't extremely careful.

Pivoting, she started for the ballroom. She stopped short when her ears picked up a scuttling sound overhead. "That's not the wind," she said out loud.

As it had her first day there, a storm pounded the manor's old walls. Thunder continued to rumble outside. When the scuttling sounds repeated, Isabella made her decision. Switching on her flashlight, she headed for the stairwell.

Pictures of a man who looked like a nineteenth-century gold miner kept her company as she climbed.

She knew it wasn't a smart thing to do, but these constant attempts to frighten her were ticking her off. So was the endless stream of questions running through her head.

Why would Katie text her instead of calling? Who in the area knew about her snake phobia? Why couldn't she find Donovan when George said he'd asked her to meet him here? Why had George been wearing the same shade of lipstick as the one used to write a warning on a napkin...?

Her ears picked up a snatch of high pitched laughter. Now that, she decided, was creepy, as creepy as walking toward it was foolish, especially with every nerve in her body screaming at her to beware. Walls might not have eyes, but something in this house made her skin crawl and her palms go damp. Time to abort.

It occurred to her as she worked her way back through the rubble that Donovan had a cell phone, too. Not always on him, but worth a shot.

She had the first three numbers pressed when a new sound underscored the storm. What started as a whisper began to ripple and swirl through the musty air.

Her heart gave several hard thumps. The feeling of being watched was acceptable, even understandable, but a full-blown hallucination was not.

And still, the sound grew.

Swinging around, Isabella backed away from a female voice that had the thunder fading into obscurity.

"Run, Isabella," it warned. "Get out of this house and don't come back. Don't let what happened to me happen to you."

And then the wail began....

"ARE YOU OUT OF YOUR mind?" Donovan shot from his truck to take her by the arms at the front gate. "Standing out here during a thunderstorm?"

In no mood to be lectured, Isabella jerked free. "I'm not in the open, and I've been pacing, not standing. George said you wanted me to meet you here. Judging from the fact that you were in town when I called, I'm guessing she lied."

"Calm down, Isabella."

"I am calm." However, she probably didn't sound it, so she raised her hands, fingers spread. "I am. I just want to know what the hell's going on. Who would think I'm naïve enough to believe that a ghost wants me to leave Darkwood Manor or die? I'll admit the dying part freaks me out, because God knows bullets and venomous snakes can kill, but the Sybil Dark impersonation's too off the wall for even my Irish blood."

Donovan regarded the distant manor. "Did the voice sound familiar?"

"No, it sounded wispy. There was an echo around the words, but, come on, Donovan, most people can change their vocal pitch to some extent. Run it through a computer and poof, instant ghost." She walked away from him, then back. "Look, I know she needs money, but I don't think George would be part of something like this."

"Did I say she would?"

Isabella thought about it. "Red lipstick's popular this season. I could also be wrong about the shade. It might not be a match for the writing on the napkin."

He intercepted her as she circled, taking her by the shoulders this time and nudging her head up until she looked straight at him. "I'll pretend I know what you're talking about, because for the most part I probably do. But no one's exempt, even if I wouldn't put George at the top of the list."

"She said you were on Dark Ridge, and you wanted me to meet you at the manor."

"All right, maybe a little closer to the top than I thought."

"It's too blatant a lie," Isabella decided. "Too obvious. Too..."

"Amateurish?"

She held his stare. "I want to go back inside. I heard noises upstairs—footsteps, I think, and maybe someone laughing, although that could have been my imagination..." A sigh slipped out. "Why are you smiling?"

"I'm relishing the moment."

For some ridiculous reason, she almost laughed. "What could there possibly be about this particular moment that you would want to relish?"

He propelled her through the front gate. "I wasn't referring to this moment. The one I'm talking about involves a twisted perp, my fists and a whole lot of blood."

Isabella started to make a reference to Aaron Dark, but stopped herself and regarded the manor instead.

"This place really would make a great hotel." In an

attempt to restore her emotional balance and his humor, she bumped his arm. "Honeymooners would love it. Great way to de-stress after the wedding."

"Yeah, nothing like a good murder mystery coupled with a mad ghost story to start a marriage."

"It's a tragic love story, Donovan. That makes it romantic."

"There's romance in the fact that Aaron threw his wife over a cliff in a fit of jealous rage?"

"Well, we'd put a slightly different spin on it, bring Sybil into the picture a little more, and—" A loud bang from the manor cut her off and had Donovan shoving her behind him.

He already had his gun out and was scanning the east side of the house.

"There." Isabella pointed through the rain to the over-grown yard.

Two people were running toward the deep woods. And the bigger one appeared to be carrying a rifle.

Chapter Twelve

"Be happy, Donovan." Isabella walked ahead of him on the muddy path. "At least be relieved. Two kids with a stick is better than two shooters with a rifle."

"They know this is private property."

"And no teen has ever ventured into forbidden territory before." Turning, she grinned at him. "Halloween's coming, remember? They wanted to scare themselves, maybe look for a place to have a party, like you probably did once upon a time."

"No comment."

Turning back, she avoided a pothole, only to wind up squishing through a mound of decomposing pine needles. "Yuck. You sent those kids home for dry clothes, Donovan. I think we should do the same—with a stop in town so I can pick up some lipstick samples."

He slanted her a canny look. "Thought you didn't suspect George?"

"I don't, but she can't be the only person who got a free-bie. I'll see what's available, take the closest color to poppy red and compare it to the writing on the napkin."

"And in doing so, hope to prove what?"

"You're the cop, you tell me."

A faint smile tugged on Donovan's lips. "It's the actual

tube we need, Isabella. Even if the colors match, we'll be no further ahead than when George showed up at your door."

"With a message from you, or so she claimed."

His smile widened. "So you do suspect her."

"No. Well, maybe. A little... I really hate this."

He surprised her by tugging on her hair, then dropping an arm over her shoulders and giving her a long, lazy kiss. "Good morning, Isabella."

It took a moment for her head to clear. "Was that a clever distraction?"

"More like self-indulgence. Don't get bogged down by the lipstick. It's possible the text messages will provide more of a clue."

"I still don't think Katie sent them—except the second one did refer to Killer." Lifting her face, she let the rain slide over her cheeks. "I just want one thing here to make sense." She gave the manor a resolute look. "We need to go through it, Donovan. There must be something inside. Signs of a struggle, speakers, wires, more hidden doors. Katie would have put up a fight."

"Not if she was chloroformed."

"What about her watch? Did it fall off accidentally, or did the man from the tunnel steal it because he's holding her somewhere?"

"You think a kidnapper would give his victim's watch away as a gift?"

"He might if his brains are below his belt. People do stupid things."

"Okay, we'll search. But first you can pick up some of those lipstick samples." At her pointed stare, he chuckled. "Any information will be helpful. I just think the text messages will tell us more."

Too cold and wet to respond, Isabella returned to her car and let him follow her to town. Frustration set in when the drugstore sales person told her the samples, the names of which she couldn't recall, were gone.

Thirty minutes later, still frustrated but finally dry in jeans, slouchy boots and a gray military-style jacket, Isabella headed up to the main lodge to wait for Donovan.

Morning adventure aside, she'd talked to him, given chase with him and, having sent the thrill-seeking teens on their way, kissed him on a rain-drenched path. It hadn't been awkward—or at least not too awkward—and all in all, she'd only thought about the night they'd spent together twenty or thirty times. Forty, tops. Yes, he looked great naked, and the sex had been the most amazing of her life, but that didn't spell love to her. Denial maybe, but not love.

The first thing Isabella saw when she entered the lobby was Robert Drake coming out of George's front office.

When he spotted her, he gestured behind him. "The phone was ringing. I thought it might be important, and there was no one here."

She smiled. "Was it?"

"What? Oh, no. Someone selling tickets."

"I see. Mr. Drake?"

Already en route to the door, the developer halted. His keys jingled at his side. "I'm late for an appointment, Ms. Ross."

"Yes, I sensed that. Is there some reason you haven't approached me about purchasing Darkwood Manor?"

His eyes came up. Sharply. "Being a hotelier, I wouldn't have thought you'd be interested in selling."

"I'm not, but being a developer, I'd have expected you to inquire."

His lips quirked at the corners. "Time isn't a thing I like to waste. I deal with those who are willing to sell first and see how far that takes me."

"I sense an underlying strategy in that sort of approach. If it were me, I'd have asked."

A dark brow rose. "But then you aren't me, are you, Ms. Ross, and sometimes a mountain simply can't be moved."

"Most times, I should think."

He stopped jingling. "On the other hand, there are ways to circumvent mountains, or if necessary, cut off the access routes leading to them."

"True," she agreed in a pleasant tone. "But I'd think twice about cutting off a mountain with the potential to erupt. The area near a volcano, specifically my grandfather, tends to suffer, and my sources tell me you've been acquiring land around Darkwood Manor recently."

"Safe land, Ms. Ross. Not the kind where people's lives might be at risk. We've all heard the wails coming from the manor. The locals believe Aaron Dark's spirit is unhappy about his house changing hands. Many believe he has the capacity for murder even in his disembodied state. Now, where you might see that as a selling feature, I see it as a potential death knell. The question is, whose death might it portend?"

With a gratuitous smile, he executed a smart turn. And walked straight into Donovan.

ACTUALLY, IT WAS GEORGE who almost got steamrolled, but only because bouncing off Donovan caused Drake to crash into her.

She would have fallen if she hadn't been clinging to Donovan's arm. As it was, she stumbled into a support beam, closed her eyes and began a slow descent to the floor.

Donovan caught her while the developer made his apologies and a speedy escape.

"Is she drunk?" Isabella asked, then remembered George's agenda and winced. "She didn't get the loan."

George's smeared lipstick created an exaggerated upward bow. "Eleven minutes," she slurred. "That's all it took for that tight-assed marmot to shoot me down. 'Place is a liability,' he said. 'You're better off bankrupt.' Good thing I didn't feel that way when I changed his dirty diapers." Her head rolled in Donovan's direction. "Where's Haden?"

"Probably at the restaurant." He raised a brow at Isabella, who took her hand.

"Was that freight train that hit me Robert Drake?"

Isabella smiled. "We were having a chat."

"We heard," Donovan said. "Can you handle her?"

"Think so. You might want to check the office. Drake was exiting as I was entering."

"Her room's through the kitchen, to the right. Get her settled. She'll sleep it off."

Easy for him to say. It took Isabella twenty minutes to coax the older woman into bed. She kept insisting that the banker should be shot and Orry Lucas with him.

"One's a marmot, the other's a rat. No, worse, he's a snake. Can't trust a damned snake…"

"I never do." After removing the red pumps, she used a throw to cover the lodge owner's splayed limbs. "Try to sleep, okay?"

George's response was a stuttering snore.

Pausing at the door with her hand on the light switch, Isabella stared at the woman's face and wondered how far a person might be willing to go if she was desperate enough.

EVEN IN BOOTS WITH THREE-INCH heels, Isabella matched him stride for stride. It was close to 4:00 p.m. and already dark as hell, but time felt short, and Donovan had learned to trust his instincts in that regard.

"I'm not accusing, I'm just saying," she maintained as

they climbed the stairs to the manor. "George needs money that I'm betting Robert Drake would be more than willing to pay."

"For what?"

She stopped on the porch. "Donovan, you told me not ten minutes ago that George told you the message she gave me came from Robert Drake, a guest who, twice in one day, has apparently taken it upon himself to answer the phone in her office. You tell me, is there any chance that George would accept money from Drake for sending me up to Darkwood under false pretenses?"

"I don't know." And that pissed him off, because he wanted to say no and mean it. "She used to slip me and my buddies six-packs of beer the year before we were legal."

He could see she was trying not to smile. "First of all, is that relevant? And second, is it supposed to be a good thing?"

"To three guys who scored two crappy beers apiece on a Friday night in Mystic Harbor, it was good enough. Denny Lucas stole his beer from the corner store, then pinned the thefts on his cousin. Orry cleaned out a lot of jail-cell toilets as payment for his so-called crimes."

"Which you evidently knew he hadn't committed." Eyes twinkling, she patted his cheek. "You were an adolescent angel, Black. I'd scold you except Aunt Mara was my George, and my friends and I preferred wine to beer. So, I'll go with the adage innocent until proven guilty, and hope the snake reference she made had nothing to do with the snake in my bed last night." Stepping around him, she gave the door a shove. "But I still don't trust Robert Drake."

"You'd be a fool if you did." Donovan's gaze swept the cobwebbed ceiling before coming to rest on the ball-room entrance. "Are you sure Katie was in there when she disappeared?"

"She called the angel on the outer molding a gargoyle, so I know she got that far."

"Does she like exploring old houses?"

"Hates it. I'm the old-house freak. It's why I scout and Katie crunches numbers."

"And does number crunching for the Corrigan-Ross Hotel Group pay well?"

She cast him a knowing look. "Quite well. My salary's higher, if that's your point. But I've been part of the business longer than her. Katie taught Accounting at a Boston business school for three years before Grandpa C convinced her to join the family team."

"Convinced or coerced?"

Irritation moved in. "You think Katie engineered her own vanishing act, don't you, that she hated her life and work, and here was a golden opportunity to ditch them both and start again."

"It's been done before."

"I'm sure it has, but Katie's not a drama queen. If she wanted out, she'd have left the business and possibly Boston as well—after she told me what she was planning to do, because she'd have known I'd help her do it." She motioned sideways but kept her eyes on his and her expression composed. "The angel's this way."

Her unruffled comeback intrigued him, almost as much as the display of Irish temper. He handed her a flashlight. "Show me where you were standing when you heard the ghostly warning."

She led him into the ballroom. "There was a creak, then about twenty seconds later, a female voice. It seemed to come from everywhere, but a wide-range speaker could simulate that effect, no problem."

He felt her tracking the line of his gaze.

"Are we looking for something in particular, Donovan?"

His lips twitched. "Can't you smell it?"

"All I smell is must, old wood and damp from the rain."

"Nothing else?"

She walked away, breathed in. "Does dust have a smell?" But as she drew alongside the window, she swung around and ran her light through the shadows. "Ghosts don't wear cheap cologne."

Donovan angled his beam over the back wall. "Looks like you're busted, Lucas."

One of the deeper shadows stirred. "Show-off," the man who'd created it muttered. "I thought you were intruders until I heard you talking." Orry raised a hand to shield his eyes. "Turn that damn thing off, Donovan. I'm not a suspect in a lineup. What are you doing here?"

"Shouldn't Isabella be asking that question?"

The deputy opened his mouth, but a sharp snap of metal had him closing it again. Only his eyes moved as he offered a shaky, "What was that?"

Isabella set her teeth. "I'm not sure what it's used for, but I'm really glad I wore boots, because it has a hard bite."

Donovan dropped his gaze. What he saw had his nerves twisting into knots of white-hot fury.

Wrapped around Isabella's ankle was a very old, very nasty foot trap.

ORRY BROUGHT AN EMERGENCY kit from the cruiser, then stood back as far as possible while Donovan examined her ankle.

Thanks to her jeans, her slouchy leather boots and the poor condition of the trap, the teeth had only penetrated deep enough to draw blood. The wounds would sting for a while, but when she considered what might have been, Isabella thought she'd gotten off lightly.

Judging from the murderous expression on his face, Donovan disagreed. He turned her foot to inspect the bloodied spots. "When was your last tetanus shot?"

"I had a booster in May. I'm covered."

"You're lucky the spring was rusty."

"And my boots have thick folds." She tried not to mourn the loss. "Aunt Mara gave them to me," she said wistfully. "They're Italian."

"Now they're ventilated," Orry called across the room.

Donovan unwrapped a roll of gauze. "Bring your flashlight over here, Lucas. My battery's dying."

"I really should be getting back."

"Did you ever tell us why you were here?"

Scowling, Orry made his way toward them. "Cousin Katie's still missing, isn't she? What do you think I was doing?"

"It looked like you were hiding in a corner," Isabella remarked.

"I explained that." Orry's neck went red. "For all I know you could've been prowlers."

"And you being the law, cowering took precedence over a potential confrontation."

"I was scoping the scene, lady. Don't tell me your fed boyfriend's never done that before... Arghh!"

To Isabella's shock, the deputy's feet shot out from under him. He landed on his back between a broken table and a twisted roll of carpet.

Donovan tied off the gauze, gave her ankle a quick inspection and, catching her chin, said, "Stay right here."

The manor had gone eerily dark over the past fifteen minutes. Tugging on her ruined boot, Isabella stood to test her ankle. The pain only climbed to her knee now. "Is he conscious?"

"He bumped his head on the table. He'll be fine."

On her hands and knees, Isabella located her flashlight. She was reaching for it when she spotted an object less than three inches from her outstretched fingers.

"Hell," she exclaimed softly and set her hand down with care. "Donovan, there's another trap over here."

She didn't realize he was beside her until he drew her to her feet. "It's for squirrels."

When Orry let out a low groan, she shook his arm. "Should we call 911?"

"It'd be the compassionate thing to do." The woozy acting sheriff rolled over, groaned again.

"Don't move," Donovan told him.

"So, I'm supposed to, what, lay here and bleed to death?" Orry probed his skull. "Sorry to disappoint you, but I'd rather crawl to my cruiser for help."

"Watch your fingers as you crawl."

Orry climbed awkwardly to his knees, yelped and pitched face-first into the remnants of a split seat cushion.

"Okay, that's it," he blustered at shaky half volume. "Whatever's going on in this loony bin, I'm done with it." The volume rose together with the quaver. "Do you hear me? All I want to do is get the hell out of here in one piece. It's her house. You don't like us being here, punish her, not me."

Despite the absurdity of his outburst, a head-to-toe chill pricked Isabella's skin. "I hate it when someone panics," she said under her breath. "It's contagious, and that sucks. Can I move now, Donovan?"

"Yeah, but slowly. You, too, Orry. Get off your stomach."

"I can't. The floor won't... I can't."

"Contagious," Isabella repeated, but took the hand Donovan held out to her.

"Walk where I walk," he said. "Grab Orry as we go past. Keep him behind you, and don't let him push."

She inspected the floor, but couldn't see anything except shadows within shadows. "I feel like we're tiptoeing through a minefield."

"We are." Donovan held her back. "Orry slipped on a bunch of ball bearings, and I've counted seven traps so far. Different sizes, different types, but all open and waiting to be sprung."

Chapter Thirteen

Orry insisted his vision was spotty, so they left the cruiser behind the manor, where he'd parked it, and drove him to the hospital clinic. A nurse there examined and rebandaged Isabella's wounds, leaving the unfortunate doctor to deal with the acting sheriff.

"Between threats and curses, Orry told me a number of people have been after him to investigate the wail we've been hearing," Isabella said to Donovan when they returned to the street.

"For *people,* read *mayor and council.* Orry knows who signs his paycheck."

"He has the makings of a great politician." She waved at the deepening mist. "So, now we trade a rainy day for a foggy night." Picking Donovan's pocket, she regarded his BlackBerry. "Wow, time flies even faster when you're not having fun. It's almost eight. No wonder I'm starving."

"The Cave it is." Donovan propelled her through the alley shortcut to Haden's restaurant.

As always, the place was crammed, a testament, Isabella supposed, to Haden's unusual menu selections and the eerie yet oddly welcoming ambiance.

She studied an oil portrait of Aaron Dark from a variety of angles. "Every time I see him, I get this tweak of familiarity." At Donovan's elevated brow, she grinned. "Nothing to do with you. With someone, though." She altered the angle of her gaze. "Right now, I'm thinking Rasputin."

"Trust me, Isabella, Aaron was no holy man."

"Neither was Rasputin. Maybe they were distantly related, and that's why people are so certain Aaron's ghost still haunts the manor. Some souls just refuse to move on."

"Refuse to or can't." Donovan drew her through the crowd toward a single empty booth. "It depends on whether you view Aaron's alleged presence as a stubborn last stand or the fate of a man condemned by a higher power."

"Could be it's a bit of both." Haden shuffled over, shoulders slumped, head bent. "Figured you'd show up when I didn't come to the manor. It wasn't cold feet," he said defensively at Donovan's faint smile. "I've got two people off sick." He gave a sheepish wave. "Aw, hell, I admit it, I was scared. Come to the kitchen, and we'll talk. Got moose on the board if you're feeling adventurous, Isabella."

"From Rocky to Bullwinkle," she murmured as she and Donovan followed Haden's broad back to the swinging door.

Someone's iPod belted out the music from *Ghostbusters* while more than a dozen kitchen staff rushed from one station to the next. The choreography of chaos fascinated her. Not a bump or spill to be seen.

They threaded their way through the culinary battlefield to Haden's cluttered office. Once there, he mopped his bushy face with a napkin and regarded his nephew.

"Got the floor plan I was gonna take to the manor right here. Now, you tell me how those inside and outside measurements add up."

Because numbers were absolutely not her thing, Isabella left Donovan and his uncle to their discussion and wandered back to the door.

Food-prep areas intrigued her. She would have settled

in to watch the action if she hadn't spied Haden's high-end printer and recalled the camera in her shoulder bag. She'd snapped at least two dozen pictures over the past several days, of structures and local vignettes Grandpa C would be impatient to see.

"Haden?" Digging out her camera, she used it to indicate the printer. "Do you mind?"

"Be my guest. Don't matter how hard I try, I can't figure the thing out."

He went back to his floor plan and an increasingly heated debate with his nephew.

Not that she thought it wise to do so, but Isabella couldn't resist taking a minute to stare at Donovan in profile. She recalled with frightening clarity the way he'd made love to her last night. A welter of sensations and feelings had exploded inside her—mind, body and, God help her, heart.

"Not ready for that one," she decided and, shutting the thought down, shucked off her jacket.

He wouldn't admit it, of course, but Grandpa C's eyes were fuzzier than they'd been a decade ago. He liked his photos big and bold, so she set the size at eight by ten and made a silent note to buy Haden a new ink cartridge.

It surprised her to discover there were more than forty shots on the card. Darkwood Manor, both whole and in segments, dominated, but there were also three pictures of Katie—those brought a pang—two of George with her high-octane brandy and one heart-stopping photo of Donovan in the fog, wearing his long black coat and an enigmatic expression that had her fanning her face with one of Haden's file folders.

The image haunted her long after she packed up the prints, so much so that she made a point of not looking at him through the dinner Haden insisted they eat in a booth barely big enough for one let alone two.

She ordered lasagna, prayed the meat wasn't squirrel or moose and knew she'd consumed too much wine when her fingertips began to go numb.

A trip to the ladies' room prevented her from jumping Donovan for dessert, but she knew—because she couldn't get her mind around anything else—that she was in deep, deep trouble where Aaron Dark's sexy descendent was concerned. Heart rules head, she reflected, exactly as Grandpa C had predicted it would.

Behind her, Lindsay banged into the washroom and stared blankly for a moment via the mirror.

"It'll come to you," Isabella promised.

When it did, the server slapped a palm over her bare wrist.

"I don't think you stole the watch." Isabella moved to the towel dispenser. "In fact, I met the man you described."

Lindsay's face lit up. "Where?"

"I bumped into him in a tunnel under Darkwood Manor."

"Seriously?" She sounded horrified. "Why were you there?"

"Because I don't believe in ghosts, I guess."

"Not even in Aaron Dark?"

"Especially not him."

Lindsay headed for a stall, but paused to look back. "I remembered something else, if it, you know, makes a difference. When I asked him where he got such a pretty watch, the guy told me he it belonged to a woman who came to Mystic Harbor a while ago. He said where she was going and who she was going with, she wouldn't be needing it."

"THAT POOR GIRL'S NEVER going to talk to me again," Isabella stated ninety minutes later. "Every time I see her, she winds up being interrogated by you and glared at by Orry."

"Orry's too busy feeling sorry for himself to glare." Donovan flicked a hand at her seat belt. "Buckle up. Fog's thick tonight."

"I wish I thought we'd learned something, but I'm pretty sure we didn't. And my guess is our mystery man will be a lot more careful about being seen now that he knows we can get into the tunnel system."

"It could have been bluster on his part, Isabella."

"Maybe, but nothing we've come up with so far explains the text messages I received, the reference to Killer, the fact that Katie's pretty much the only person who calls me Bella…"

"The snake in your bed, the gunshots, the knife or the lipstick message. Let it go for a few hours," Donovan advised. "Keep covering the same ground, and you'll drive yourself crazy. I promise, we'll figure this thing out."

Because he was right, she controlled her frustration and tested her fingertips for sensation while he navigated the slippery road. All normal. Unsure whether to be relieved or disappointed, she wiggled all her fingers. "Guess I'm not drunk."

"Did you think you were?"

"I wanted to jump you at the restaurant. In the sheriff's office, too, but that's a little weird and probably has something to do with you being a fed." Reaching over, she played with the ends of his hair. "Does that last part bruise your ego?"

"Depends on where this ends up."

It was an opening she simply couldn't resist.

When he cut the engine outside her cabin, fog immediately cloaked his truck. She couldn't see the lights of the lodge or even her own front door. But she could see

Donovan, and she wanted him. Wanted to feel his hands on her skin, on her breasts. Wanted him inside her.

A smile bloomed as he lifted her across the gearshift so she could straddle his lap.

She let her lips brush his while her hips moved against him. "Seems I'm caught between a rock and a hard place, Black. If we say the hard place is behind me, then I'm liking the rock."

And tangling her fingers in his hair, she set her mouth on his.

HE DIDN'T LOVE HER; IT wasn't possible. He'd guarded his heart for too many years to let love happen.

It was lust, he told himself, a hormonal backlash born of self-denial. And one helluva hot woman.

The night had come and gone in a sexual blur. He should have left hours ago. But already the first traces of dawn were stealing through the layers of mist that clung to the rocks and trees, and here he was, half dressed and not entirely sure where his keys had landed.

He sat on the sofa with his bare feet propped on a low table, drank coffee he'd foolishly brewed and stared at the moody black outline of Darkwood Manor perched so high on the ridge that it escaped the encroaching ocean fog.

Locals insisted that Aaron's virulent presence attracted only the bitter forces of nature. Black fog might stick, but the gentler autumn version didn't have a chance.

Setting his head on the sofa back, Donovan turned his mind to Isabella's situation.

An old suit and bullets. Rattraps and more bullets. Ghostly warnings and knives. An arrow in the front door, an attempted abduction, a note written in red lipstick. Two text messages from a missing cousin whose boyfriend's name was Killer. A mystery man in the passageway under the manor. Orry hiding inside the ballroom yesterday. Darlene sneaking into the sheriff's office through the back door.

Darlene worked for Gordie Tallahassee. Gordie was a Realtor. Robert Drake was a developer. Drake was staying at George's lodge. George needed money.

Isabella's ex had purchased Darkwood, then died in a car crash and left the manor to her. The manor had inside-outside dimensions that Haden swore, and he agreed, didn't add up.

Sleep-deprived and buzzed on sex, Donovan's brain would have imploded if he'd let it. But he'd been trained to compartmentalize, so he did. Shoved everything he had into boxes and jammed tight lids on them.

Most of them anyway. No box could hope to contain his feelings for Isabella.

The cell phone on his waistband vibrated. At five minutes shy of 6:00 a.m., it couldn't be good news.

He regarded the screen, then picked up.

More than the words on the other end registered, but he kept his muscles loose and his expression neutral while he absorbed the information.

He knew she was behind him. He'd felt her come into the room. He could smell her hair and skin. That tropical rain-forest scent had been driving him out of his mind since he'd met her.

When the call ended, she leaned over and ran her hands down his chest. Her hair grazing his cheeks kindled the still-simmering embers from last night.

"You might as well tell me the bad news, Donovan, because I know that wasn't Haden you were swearing at."

"I was swearing at the information, not the person."

She pressed her cheek to his temple. "And the reason was?"

"I had a friend check out the text messages you received

from your cousin. Local cell towers can give the general direction of outgoing calls." Because face-to-face was better, he stood, took her by the arms and held her gaze with his. "They were local, Isabella. Both messages originated in Mystic Harbor."

WALKING AHEAD OF HER, Donovan gestured at the manor floor. "Point your light down. This hallway's more treacherous than the ballroom."

A wire snagged her jeans. "I noticed. Any ball bearings or rusty traps?"

"Not so far."

"That's a plus. The big kitchen's to your left." She ducked under an enormous cobweb. "Look, I know you're thinking that Katie and Killer are doing something together, but you're wrong."

"What I'm thinking is that someone's gone to a great deal of trouble to frighten you. That suggests a large payoff to me."

"As in I sell the manor, and the person who brought that about reaps the benefits?"

"Yes."

"In whose fantasy world does abduction fall under the heading 'scare tactic'? There's also the little matter of bullets, as in the ones that were fired at you and Orry on the ridge, and again at you and me in the tunnel under the manor. The knife's borderline if someone skilled threw it, but a poisonous snake in the bed of a phobic person is just plain—"

"Cruel."

When he reached back to touch her cheek, her vexation melted into a sigh. "Katie wouldn't be part of anything this sick. Even Killer couldn't talk her into it."

"Fair enough." He ran the outline of a double doorway

with his flashlight. "But what about Killer alone, or, more specifically, without Katie's cooperation?"

Isabella started to answer, then closed her mouth and looked away.

"Not sure, huh?"

She squeezed past a packing crate. "Pretty sure I don't like you in your cop hat right now."

A small grin crossed his lips. "In that case, I might as well go for broke and ask about your cousin's relationship with your ex."

"Katie and David?" Too stunned to be annoyed, Isabella stared at him. "You think there was something between them?"

"I'm wondering if Katie might have liked him more than she let on."

"Donovan, the only thing Katie liked about David was his car. He had a 1960s cherry-red Corvette Stingray. I don't mean to make her sound callous, but she probably mourned the loss of the car more than she did David."

"So she wouldn't be feeling hostile toward you."

"To what end? David's dead."

"He left Darkwood Manor to you, Isabella. Whatever you choose to do with the house, the several hundred acres of land it sits on is worth a considerable amount of money."

She made a flat hand motion. "Forget it. First of all, I repeat, Katie couldn't stand David. Second, David was a one-woman man. Quirky, yes, but not the sharing kind. He wouldn't have gotten involved with another woman while we were dating, and he definitely wouldn't have done it with someone who was already in a relationship."

Donovan's smile widened slightly. "Put your dagger down—that's not where I was going. Jealousy," he said at her mistrustful glare. "I want to know if you think Katie could have been jealous of your relationship with David Gimbel."

"Jealous enough to do all this? Answer's no, Black, in uppercase letters."

But a tiny niggle of doubt crept in to irritate her. Squashing it, she took a deep breath and fought for patience.

"I accept that questions are part of your everyday life, but you're way off track with this. Yes, Katie and I occasionally wanted the same guy—back in high school and college where everything sex-related came down to steamy looks, ripped bodies and adolescent fantasies, but those days are long gone, like my tolerance for this conversation."

He leaned a shoulder on the wall. "So now wouldn't be a good time for me to tell you you're beautiful when you're angry?"

Patience lost the battle to exasperation. Kicking a chunk of fallen plaster aside, Isabella strode up to him, batted his flashlight arm aside and grabbed the front of his shirt with both hands. "You haven't begun to see angry yet, pal."

Yanking his mouth onto hers, she gave him a kiss that rocked her as deeply as she hoped it rocked him.

She ended it by pulling away and letting her eyes glitter. "Slag my cousin's character again, and you'll see Irish lightning bolts courtesy of Jimmy the Hammer Corrigan, aka Grandpa C, who taught me how to swing a mean right at any adversary I can see coming."

"As opposed to the ones who use chloroform and attack from the rear." Donovan's eyes glittered now, which lightened her mood considerably. As was the case with misery, it appeared edgy also liked company. It might have been intriguing to watch the fireworks unfold. Unfortunately, the shadowy halls of Darkwood Manor weren't conducive to romance.

Could be with time and effort, Isabella acknowledged,

but for the moment a murky, vaguely malevolent atmosphere prevailed.

She made herself release his shirt, then felt her stomach seize as a creak that read like a screech emanated from the room ahead.

"It's a torture chamber around here. I'm picturing Aaron Dark on a tear with a butcher knife."

Donovan took her hand. "Aaron didn't dismember his wife."

And ghosts shouldn't make ancient floorboards groan, but that didn't make her feel any better.

The gloom thickened the deeper they ventured into the manor. Their flashlights sliced a path through the heart of it but did little to reveal what lurked on either side.

A second creak reached them when they entered the kitchen. "That wasn't the floor."

"I think there's a door beside that big stone fireplace to our right. I remember it from the first day, when I was too worried about Katie's disappearance to be scared. There's also a window on the back wall, but it's shuttered and stuck." She touched his arm before he could move. "I heard a footstep."

"Stay behind me," Donovan instructed. "Shine your light in the opposite direction."

Isabella's heart sounded like thunder in her ears. She turned a circle in Donovan's wake, certain the eyes she felt watching her would reveal themselves in her beam.

"Forget being thrown from a cliff. If I'd been Sybil Dark and forced to live here with a madman, I'd have jumped."

"Maybe she did."

"You're such a comfort, Black."

Charred fragments of wood from the hearth littered the floor. One of them resembled the clawlike bones of a human hand.

Lovely thought, she reflected and stepped over it. "Are we anywhere near the window?"

"More than near. I've got the latch, but you're right—it's jammed."

Something brushed Isabella's leg. She snapped her light down, then around in a quick half circle.

There was nothing except dirt and bits of wood.

A moment later, she caught a movement in her peripheral vision. She knew it wasn't Donovan because he was heading for the pantry.

The glow at the rim of her beam revealed a section of counter inset with a wide farm sink. Through the layered shadows, she made out a tail as something leaped from counter to neighboring hearth.

When she swung her flashlight across, two yellow eyes appeared. They stared at her, unblinking.

It took several seconds for the silhouette of an enormous black cat to emerge from the inky backdrop.

Relief chased by curiosity shivered through her. "Was it you I saw in that hidden room a few days ago?" She held out a hand to let the animal sniff her. "I bet you know all the ins and outs of this house, don't you? If you could talk, we'd be set."

As if it understood, the cat meowed and jumped from the hearth. Isabella noticed a tag dangling from its collar and wondered if it had a name. Or more telling, an owner.

As long shots went, the prospect seemed far-fetched, but Aunt Mara's gray Persian followed her everywhere, so it might be worth a shot.

Calling to Donovan, she followed the feline into a narrow hallway that crooked toward an even narrower stairwell. One set of stairs went up, the other down. Both looked intimidating in the dark.

She had no idea which way the cat had gone, but because

this was an area of the house she hadn't yet explored, she played her light in all directions.

She didn't realize her palms had gone damp until the sensation of being watched made her stomach quiver. To some extent, the feeling was omnipresent; however, at times it became a tangible thing, like an icy finger trailing up and down her spine.

Her heart thudded as panic tap-danced inside. Before it could take root, she backed away from the stairwells and carefully down the hall.

All this for a cat that probably had nothing to do with anything and simply liked to wander around old buildings hunting for mice.

Her heels created the only true sound in the corridor. Imagination did the rest, right down to the heavy breathing that had to be her own.

Or not.

"Isabella…"

The man's voice was a mere echo in the shadowy air.

"Crap," she swore in a clenched undertone. She continued walking backward, her eyes sweeping the darkness.

"Are you frightened?" he whispered. "Are you ready to submit? Or will you follow the tragic path of your predecessor?"

She found her voice and enough resentment to slap back. "I don't have a predecessor who relates to this house." Unless he was referring to Katie. "I also don't believe in ghosts, so whoever you are, you won't get what you want this way."

His eerie little laugh had the effect of nails on a blackboard. She'd returned Donovan's backup gun to him. Why had she done that? She groped for the doorway behind her.

"What I want, Isabella, is a thing only you can give me. And I'll have it back, because no one takes what's mine."

The voice lost its eerie edge and deepened to a growl. "Do you hear me? No one ever takes what's mine."

Movement erupted within the shadows, a flash of arm followed by a glint of black metal.

Something struck the floor. A muffled cry was immediately superseded by the hiss of an angry cat.

Her desperate hand finally located the door. Yanking it open, she ran across the threshold, through the kitchen and into the pantry.

"Donovan!"

She still had her flashlight and, whirling, searched the room. The shelves that stretched from floor to ceiling leaned menacingly toward her. She swore she could hear the man breathing, could still hear his voice, a silky whisper of sound.

Fear pulsed through her like a thousand squirming snakes.

"Black?" she tried again.

She spotted his flashlight, lying on the broken floor tiles not twelve inches from a partly open section of wall.

But there was no sign of Donovan.

Chapter Fourteen

She was going to play with a cat?

Donovan suspected the tangle of thoughts in his head had distorted Isabella's words. He started to respond, but as he turned, he knocked one of the shelves he'd been examining and heard a quiet click.

Both the shelves and the wall on which they were mounted moved. A careful tug revealed a two-by-six-foot opening. A ladder staircase descended into full, fathomless black.

He tested the frame several times. Interesting. In a house riddled with rusty metal fittings and warped joists, this hidden door opened without a single creak.

He ran his flashlight over the hinges. Someone had used enough oil on them to lubricate three doors, enough to come and go in silence, the way a ghost would.

Although the opening intrigued him, first and foremost he needed to stop Isabella from chasing a cat around the manor—because he couldn't see this being the only hidden door the would-be specter used.

He was turning for the kitchen when he spotted the shadow of a man on the kitchen wall.

He reached for his gun. The shadow halted. Donovan crept forward; however, while the oiled hinges might be silent, the floorboards were anything but. The one beneath him groaned loudly. Alerted, the shadow backpeddled and vanished through a side entrance. Swearing, Donovan followed him out.

The day's premature twilight had bled into a moonless night. Mist twined about his legs as he slowed to determine direction.

The shadow man likely knew the surrounding woods. He'd have had his escape route memorized.

The bushes rustled. With his gun pointed skyward, Donovan listened.

The wind was negligible, but the ocean was a constant series of crashes above an omnipresent roar, tall waves tumbling over rocks then slamming into the cliff below.

Another shudder of leaves and limbs reached him. He jogged along something resembling a path. Ahead and to his right, the bushes vibrated, then gave a mighty shake.

He stopped, watched, waited until the foliage burst apart. And snapping his gun down, took aim at the figure that sprang from the black void inside.

BRAIN OVERLOAD. ISABELLA had it in spades. If Donovan, a trained professional, couldn't make sense of what was happening, she held out little hope of finding the answers herself.

He'd spotted a shadow, given chase and come within a heartbeat of killing a deer spooked out of the bushes by well, by whoever had been creeping through the manor, she assumed.

Meanwhile, she'd been threatened yet again, not by a woman this time, but a man. She estimated she'd been less than five feet away from him when the cat she'd been trailing had tripped him up.

Kudos to the cat, whoever it belonged to.

Back at George's lodge, Donovan talked to a cop friend

while Isabella sat on the staircase and contemplated whether to call Grandpa C or wait one more day.

She tried Killer's number, and got the same tired response. She left yet another message and broke the connection.

The lobby had grown noisy over the past thirty minutes. Seven round poker tables took up half the floor space. Robert Drake was there, sequestered in a dark corner. Gordie Tallahassee had arrived flushed and breathless fifteen minutes ago. Orry was conspicuously absent.

Darlene stood by the reception desk with an unlit cigarette between her fingers and a scowl on her face. Her gaze flicked from Donovan to the tables, and then to the staircase.

"Have you seen my mother?" she called across the room.

"Smoke break outside."

Darlene strolled toward the staircase, lighting her cigarette as she came. "You're looking a tad shaky tonight, Isabella. Manor getting to you?"

"Only as it relates to my cousin's disappearance."

"At the risk of sounding like a broken record, you're a fool for not selling."

"Because tampering with Aaron Dark's house will piss him off? Sorry, not biting."

"I believe your former boyfriend said something similar a week or so before he died."

"David drove a powerful vehicle too fast on a slippery road, overshot a hard turn and crashed. I doubt if a nineteenth-century ghost would know enough about twentieth-century cars to have brought that about. Aaron's more into wails and whispered threats. Oh, yeah, and warning notes." She summoned a pleasant smile. "That's a pretty shade of lipstick you're wearing. Not poppy red, I notice."

Darlene took a drag from her cigarette, matched Isabella's

smile. "I like the darker tones myself. If I were you, sweetie, I'd consider—"

The front door opened and Orry swaggered in. Darlene cursed and swiveled away when George pushed through from the kitchen.

"What?" she demanded at Isabella's raised brows. "I've got a moron on one side and a mother with a guilt whip on the other. Get your butt pinched a few times and see how eager you are to serve beer to a bunch of baboons. Stay out of my face, Orry," she warned the approaching deputy. "You, too, Donovan." This as her cousin came up from behind. "I'm not in the mood for a showdown of words."

"Makes two of us."

"Three," Isabella said.

"Four," Orry snarled. "Here." He thrust something into Isabella's hand. "I found this at the manor before you and Dead-eye Dick appeared, and I wound up with a concussion."

Isabella regarded the earring in her palm. It was a simple white-and-yellow gold bonding of the letters *C* and *R*. Problem was...

"This isn't mine."

Orry's snarl became a sneer. "It says CR, lady, as in Corrigan-Ross."

She gave her head a shake, glanced at Donovan beside her. "It isn't mine."

"Katie's?"

"It goes with the watch."

Donovan picked up the earring by its stud back. "Looks like we'll be making another trip to the manor."

"I DON'T SEE WHY *WE* has to include me." Orry glowered at the rain-drenched manor. "There are a hundred better things

I could be doing at three in the afternoon than letting you drag me into a house that hates non-Dark humans."

Donovan cut the engine, scanned the blackened windows. "Houses don't hate," he said in a distracted tone.

"What's left of Aaron does."

"He's in good company."

"You're a real comedian, Donovan." Slamming the truck door, Orry darted under the overhang. "The only reason people and ghosts like you is because they think you're so cool. Well, I get my share of attention too."

"Yeah, I saw the lipstick on your collar." Donovan pocketed his keys. "How'd your wife feel about that?"

The acting sheriff's cheeks mottled. "None of your damned business. Are the traps still here?"

"Far as I know. I didn't see any around the perimeter of the room. Stay out of the main part and we should be good." At the ballroom entrance, he repositioned his gun. "Where was the earring?"

"Ten feet ahead, to the left of that headless, armless thing."

"That would be a replica of the *Venus de Milo.*"

Orry's lip curled up. "No accounting for taste, is there?" A loud snap brought him to attention. "What was that?"

"One less trap to worry about. There's nothing between us and Venus, Orry."

"There was nothing around Venus, either, except bits of plaster, a ton of dead bugs and one shiny earring." The deputy dug in. "This is ridiculous. Isabella says that earring belongs to her cousin. Am I arguing? She insists something happened to the woman. Fine, I'm on board with that. No idea where cousin Katie's car went, but hey, still on board. Car'll turn up. Probably in Florida where she drove it after she staged her disappearance, but who am I to question the woman's motives? Oh, wait, I'm the acting sheriff, and while chasing the odd wild goose might come with the territory, I'd rather chase a local goose than one from another frigging state."

Something akin to guilt snaked through Donovan's stomach. Hadn't he thought the same thing at one time? Thought it even when Isabella swore it wasn't possible?

Orry swept an arm across the floor. "See? Nothing else there."

Going down on one knee, Donovan measured the distance to the wall and considered the possibilities.

"Right, we came, we saw, let's go." However, in his rush to exit, Orry stepped on something that squealed. He emitted a scream of his own and bounced off Donovan's shoulder and crashed into the wall.

"I see how that stupid bust thing lost her head and arms." He levered upright. "This house is booby-trapped from top to bottom —and I'm the real boob for letting you drag me in here when… What?" he demanded as Donovan flicked a hand at his holster.

"Gun."

The deputy's eyes wheeled from side to side. "Why?"

"Because we're going down."

Orry leaped to his haunches, spied the hidden opening and drew back. "What is that?"

"A doorway."

"With no knob. And stairs that go down. Into nothing."

A faint smile crossed Donovan's lips as Orry added a firm, "I'll watch your back from here."

Since he'd be more of a hindrance than a help in any case, Donovan stepped through the panel opening. "Don't let the eyes in the portraits spook you, Orry. They only look like they're watching your every move."

After checking his gun, he disappeared into the dark.

"YOU KNOW WHY HE DIDN'T want you to go." Haden scooted the soup chef away from her simmering pot for a taste. "Needs more onions," he pronounced. "Look what happened last time you were there. Almost got your ankle hacked off. And you just know by the way Orry was dragging his feet all day that he'd be more than happy to push you into another trap if it meant he could avoid it. You're better off here at the restaurant, sampling my new dishes and printing pictures for your granddad."

A vexed Isabella didn't want to do either thing.

"Are there many in Mystic Harbor who can trace their lineage directly to Aaron Dark or his sister?"

Haden made a note about the soup while he circled his desk. "Not as directly as the four of us, no, but there's plenty can claim a distant family tie. And of course Sybil had people, too, uncles and cousins and such. Some of them get a little huffy at the suggestion they have no claim to Darkwood Manor. It could be by today's laws they have a point. But the manor was sold off long ago, so really the whole question's a tempest in a teapot. Darkwood's yours until you decide it's not."

As its current owner, Isabella wanted to be there right now, searching. However, when she'd suggested as much to Donovan, he'd kissed her and turned her brain to mush. If part of her resented that, another part had to admit the man knew how to get around her—and he'd used the knowledge to full advantage.

The whirring printer spit out the remainder of her Mystic Harbor photos. She was lining them up when something about the last one captured her attention.

She'd taken this particular shot the night George had joined her on the rock outside her cabin. Darkwood Manor loomed on the ridge, but it wasn't the house she saw when she looked closer. It was the trees, or more accurately, a figure secreted within the trees.

If she hadn't done eight by tens, Isabella doubted she would have noticed anything unusual even with the aid of a nearly full moon. But the larger size revealed more than a figure among the branches and limbs. It showed a figure holding a knife. Preparing to throw that knife.

After enlarging the relevant segment, she held it up to the light. "That's not good," she decided. And with only the briefest hesitation, she went to find Haden.

"I SHOULD'VE KNOWN." The big man gave his head a resounding smack, followed by a shake that sent raindrops scattering in every direction. "Girl's always been a malcontent, always wanted more, wanted out. Still, I shouldn't have been so abrupt on the phone."

To Isabella's amazement, he opened the outer office door with caution. "Woo-oo, Darlene, it's Haden. You busy?"

On the sidewalk behind him, Isabella nudged his spine. "I hate to rush you, but I'm standing in a waterfall out here."

He didn't budge. "If you don't know it yet, knives aren't the only things Darlene can throw. Girl's got a mean temper."

"She's not alone." Out of patience, Isabella squeezed past him into the messy reception area. "There's no point hiding, Darlene. The shop owner next door told us you were here."

A wisp of smoke curling out of the supply closet gave her away. When Isabella opened the door, Donovan's cousin swished past. "Bug off, sweetheart, I'm on my break."

"In the closet."

"I like privacy."

"You like throwing knives, too." Isabella dangled the

incriminating photo twelve inches from the other woman's face. "Care to explain this, ace?"

Darlene blew an insolent stream of smoke. "No. Now beat it before I call Orry and have you arrested for trespassing."

Haden snorted. "Can't trespass in a public office during business hours." He shook a meaty finger at her. "You threw a knife at Isabella. Don't deny it—the proof's right there in her hand. You got eyes like Donovan's and an arm the Sox would love to have under contract. Now you sit down at your desk, and tell us why you did what you did."

Lips thinning, Darlene exhaled smoke through her nose. "You were never in any real danger," she said in a controlled tone.

"Want me to throw a knife and see how you feel?"

"My guess is I'd feel blood. There was no chance of that for you."

"Then why did you do it?"

"Because he...I..." Air hissed out from between her teeth. "Damn you and your camera. I never intended to hit you, only to shake you up a bit."

"I figured that much." Isabella absorbed her stony stare. "Who's *he?*"

"If you're smart, you'll let it go."

"Does he have some kind of hold on you?"

"What? No." But she deflated slightly. "I'm not sure what he has, that's the problem. More malice than I thought. Not as much. Somewhere in between. All I know is that he wants you to sell the manor and go back to Boston."

"Sell to who?"

A cynical smile stole across the other woman's lips. "Who wants the property most?"

"Robert Drake."

"Bingo."

"Is Drake your partner?"

"Hardly."

A sigh escaped. "No, I didn't think it would be that simple."

"Why not?" a perplexed Haden demanded.

"Because the answer's too obvious. Anyway, I picture Drake more like a vulture. Let someone else do the dirty work. He'll swoop in when the killing's done."

"Killing! My God, Darlene!" The blood drained from Haden's normally ruddy cheeks. "You wanted Isabella dead?"

"I didn't want her anything but gone." She took a deep drag. "Money was my goal. If I could help make a sale happen, I'd get a nice fat payoff through my partner." She moved a shoulder in Isabella's direction. "You're right about Drake, though. He's a scavenger. Didn't want to soil his hands directly, but he let it be known to anyone who'd listen that he was in the market for land. Although he's bought some of it outright, one conversation with your grandfather confirmed that acquiring yours would call for a different tack."

A gust of wind blew rain against the office window. When Darlene's gaze traveled to the street, Isabella drew a controlled breath. "Did your partner do something to my cousin? Is he capable of—" She had to force the word out "—murder?"

"Sixty-four-thousand-dollar questions… Oh, Haden, for the love of God, stop looking at me like I'm the Boston Strangler and Jack the Ripper rolled into one. I was approached. I said yes. I thought we were going to scare her off. You know, do the woo-woo thing until she either bought into the ghost story or just got sick of being harassed. Either way, ka-ching, major sale." Darlene screwed the heel of her hand into her forehead. "It got off track somehow. I didn't mean for it to, but I swear, that deal in the tunnels and the attempted abduction—nothing to do with me." In an unexpected and somewhat unnerving move, she snagged Isabella's wrist and squeezed. "You want my advice, you'll get the hell out of Mystic Harbor. If I don't know how far he'll go, no one does."

Isabella regarded her through the haze of expelled smoke. "Give us a name, Darlene."

Her eyes touched briefly on the building across the street. Drawing back, she crushed out the cigarette she'd smoked right down to its white filter.

Under the glare of florescent light, something about the lipstick smear on the end struck a chord in Isabella's memory. She was good with colors, always had been. Darlene didn't wear poppy red, she wore a deeper, richer shade of Bordeaux.

Like the lipstick Donovan had seen on Orry Lucas's collar.

Chapter Fifteen

Donovan hadn't intended to goad the deputy into accompanying him, yet thirty seconds after he entered the tunnel system, Orry hastened into view, gun drawn and looking thoroughly out of sorts.

"I hate you," he announced, and pushed past with a belligerent, "Let's get this done."

Donovan noticed that he kept his teeth together, probably so they wouldn't crack when they chattered.

"I should have my head examined. I don't like dark, wet places. I also don't have to prove a thing to you or anyone else."

Because Orry refused to, Donovan brought up the rear, staying two feet behind him at all times. His gaze skimmed over the rocks above. "I didn't drag you down here," he remarked at length. "You could've stayed in the ballroom."

"And after being observed and deemed disposable, wound up getting whacked by whoever planted those traps. No thanks, pal." He used his gun to draw an arc. "Do you know where we are?"

"Yeah, in a passageway, thirty minutes from the bottom of the stairs we took to get here."

Thirty minutes stretched to sixty, then to ninety. Donovan lost track of time and direction. As if sensing the last thing, Orry, who'd been uncommonly quiet, twitched a shoulder.

"How many passageways are down here? Feels like a thousand."

Donovan's lips curved. "Close to a hundred, anyway."

"So, armed with that knowledge and having only two flashlights and a couple of guns between us, you figure there's a snowball's chance in hell of us, one, finding Isabella's cousin and or, two, getting out of here before we're eighty years old?"

He sounded more jumpy than angry, Donovan noted. "I told you, we're looking for a man." He watched the water dripping from an overhead rock turn into a thin but steady stream. "The one Haden's server Lindsay met in the Raven last week."

"Right. The phantom no one else has seen. Oh, no, sorry, Isabella saw him. You mentioned that little subterranean episode a few days ago, didn't you?"

"Did I?"

"Someone did," Orry snapped. "Point is, her seeing him is hardly confirmation that the guy exists, since Ms. Ross also claims to have a missing cousin that no one except her—and I'm including you here—has laid eyes on."

"Thought you believed her about Katie."

"I said I was on board with her disappearance. I only believe what I see for myself." His feet stopped moving. "Or, uh, hear."

Donovan's eyes came up.

The acting sheriff spun. "I heard a splash, a distinct splash—as in there's someone down here with us."

"Quiet."

Orry stopped speaking, but his breath rattled in and out.

"Wait here." As Donovan moved deeper into the tunnel, he heard another splash. When he looked back, he saw Orry slogging along behind him.

"Can I help it if there are puddles everywhere?" the frazzled man demanded.

Letting it go, Donovan projected his senses forward, into the heart of the underground maze.

They'd been creeping downhill for the past half hour. The air was cold and damp as hell. Whoever Isabella had seen, he couldn't be living here. So what was he doing, coming and going from the manor, giving Katie's watch to a stranger and shooting at people in the dark?

He put the last question on hold and a hand on Orry's chest.

Neither of them moved. Water trickling from the overhead rocks provided the only sound.

"Maybe it was a rat," Orry suggested in a hoarse voice.

But Donovan didn't think so. He kept his gun up and his eyes on the shadows that shifted in the glow of his flashlight.

Twenty seconds ticked by. Thirty. Finally, there was a subtle slosh. It came from directly ahead.

"Going for it," Donovan said and took off before Orry could react.

Someone's feet immediately began to slap on the soggy ground. He heard a curse and a grunt followed by more wet pounding. The feet turned left. So did Donovan. The water got deeper, the ground more treacherous.

Was he gaining? No way to tell. But he had a belt light and sharp eyes, and the satellite passages appeared to be diminishing, as if the system was forming a bottleneck.

Far ahead he spied a ladder. A man ran toward it at full speed.

Gotcha, bastard, Donovan thought and shouted a warning.

The man hesitated, then seemed to panic and leaped for

the rungs. His hands caught the sides only to be torn away when Donovan tackled him into the muddy wall.

Bared teeth gleamed within a framework of facial scruff. Dark, curly hair hung in his eyes. He made a gagging sound as he endeavored to pry Donovan's forearm from his throat.

One fist went for his captor's ribs; his knee took aim at the groin. Neither connected. Catching his wrist, Donovan swung him around and plowed him face-first into the wall.

"You're wasting your time, pal," the man bit out. "My hands are empty, and I'm not on parole."

"Good to know. What's your name?"

"Screw you."

"Figured as much. You know I'm going to haul you in, right?"

"For what? Like I said, empty hands."

"You attempted to assault a federal officer. Since I didn't identify myself when I nabbed you, I'll let that one go." He loosened his grip as he spoke. The man held for a moment, then twisted around and tried to ram his balled fist into Donovan's throat. Grinning, Donovan offset the blow and spun him back into the wall.

"Hell," the man swore. "You did that on purpose."

"Must've lost my grip." He wrenched the guy's arm up a little higher. "Okay, friend, now we're talking attempted assault coupled with trespassing. Anything else you'd like to talk about while we're here?"

The man's breath puffed out like an enraged bull. "I don't want to get mixed up in this."

"You already are."

"Not the way you're thinking."

"If you know what I'm thinking, then you know what's going down at the manor. You want to go with it, that's your choice. But one way or another I'll get to the truth, and when I do, I'm guessing assault and trespassing won't be the only charges on your plate."

"I don't…ahhh…all right, I hear you. We're talking deal, right? I say what I know, you let me disappear."

He gave the guy another shove. "You think?"

"No, but you better, fed, and fast, or you and that pretty rabbit—er, lady, you like so much might not be around much longer."

Donovan's muscles clenched. "Five seconds," he warned.

The man grimaced. "Yeah, okay, you don't have to tear my arm off. I don't know who the guy is, but I saw him twice when he didn't think anyone was around."

"What did you see him doing?"

"Skulking in that big room next to the front entrance. Once, he was poking through the junk. Second time, he put something down. Or picked it up. I couldn't tell which, and I wasn't about to ask."

"You're afraid of him."

The man wheezed out a laugh. "Damn right I am. You would be, too, if you watched him for a while. Guy's a walking creep show. Maybe not so you'd see in an ordinary day, but when the spotlight's off, look hard, and you won't wanna hang around."

"Did you recognize him?"

"Well, I don't exactly get out a lot, now, do I?"

"You got out long enough to give a watch to a woman at the Raven."

"Oh, well, that."

"Yeah, that."

"I found the watch—in that big room."

"Before or after you saw the creep poking around?"

"Before, I think. I wasn't keeping a journal. Pretty sure it was before, though. I get tired of living like a mole, so sometimes I go up into the house. Took a stroll one night, and there it was, ticking away on the floor. I had a hankering for a beer and a need for food, so I took a chance and went to town. Saw a fox, wanted some company, started to chat."

"And then?"

He managed to shrug. "Lady wasn't as willing as I thought."

"Can you describe the guy in the ballroom?"

"Oh, come on. You think I got that close? He was a guy, and he stuck to the shadows. It isn't hard to do in that house."

"If you didn't see him clearly, what made you think he was a creep?"

"The way he bopped."

Donovan's patience was wearing thin. "Define *bopped*."

"I can't explain it better than that. First time I saw him, he bopped his head like he was listening to an iPod. Maybe he was. He bopped, and then he pulled a gun. Bopped and pretended to shoot it. Second time, he had two guns, and he was making a rat-a-tat sound. The time between—"

"You said you only saw him twice," Donovan interrupted.

"*Saw* him twice, yeah. Heard him once. That was the time between, when you and your lady came into the tunnels. Man, for a big place, there was a lot of traffic in one small area. Anyway, there I was, minding my own business, when all of a sudden I heard voices. Yours and the pretty lady's. I stopped to wait, and bam, bam, bam, a bunch of bullets flew past my head. I plastered myself to the wall, flat as I could. I heard someone running past, going one way. A few seconds later, he was going back the other way, jabbering about getting something that used to be his back. Then you came along. I heard more shots, but damned if I cared who was firing them. I just wanted out. So I ran, and that's when me and the lady crossed paths. I shoved her aside and beat it into the nearest cave."

"Did you notice anything about the guy other than he bops, sticks to the shadow and likes to play with guns?"

"Told you before, I mind my own whenever and wherever possible. I see him again, though, I'll slip him a note that he was shooting at a fed down here."

Donovan's eyes narrowed. "What do you mean, he was shooting at a fed?"

"Mean what I said. Guy was gunning for you that day."

Hauling the man from the wall, Donovan regarded him in shadowy relief. "Are you saying he wanted to kill me and not Isabella?"

"Look, I can only tell you what I heard, and the clearest thing I heard was him swearing as he thundered past me that he'd get the bastard who was with her if it was the last thing he did." The man displayed dull teeth. "Whoever he is, it sounds like he's planning to get that something he wants back over your dead body."

"WHY WOULD HE DO THIS, Isabella?" Haden repeated again and again. "I've known him for years. He's always wanted status, but you heard Darlene. He's gone from Jekyll to Hyde a couple times lately."

"Yes, I know." And it frightened her.

When she pulled the car keys from her pocket, Haden caught the folded family tree that came out with them before it landed in a puddle. "He's not a Dark. Pretty sure not, anyway."

"Haden, insanity isn't limited to the Dark family." Isabella slid behind the wheel. "Anyway, Darlene only said she didn't know what he might be capable of, not that he was a raving lunatic."

"Guess not." The big man started to wring the folded paper, thought better of it and smoothed the creases on his bench-sized lap. "Are you sure you can't reach Donovan?"

"I've tried three times." She handed him her cell. "If he's gone into the tunnels, the signal won't get through, but he can't stay down there forever."

She refused to visualize the worst-case scenario.

Haden went back to twisting on the family tree. "There's an ugly bunch of black clouds hanging over Dark Ridge, and lightning out on the water. I saw it flash. Thunder'll be rolling in with it."

Around them, the trees had already begun to bend as the wind gained strength.

"It's gonna get nasty," he predicted. "Rain on its own's no problem, but thunderstorms give me heebie-jeebies." His shoulders hunched. "Did you know that Aaron's son, the one who died young, was a chemist? Some say he was trying to concoct a cure for what he called right-hemisphere deficiency, and that he tested it out on his brother's youngest daughter, who was supposed to be touched."

Isabella regarded the boiling clouds, shivered and turned the wipers on high. "Any success with that?"

"I doubt it. He was only in his early thirties when his niece found him dead. Heart attack in his sleep, the doctor said, but there's those who don't believe that."

"Haden…"

He raised his hands. "I haven't grown a third eye, Isabella. I'm just saying what is. Plenty of people in town figure my head's screwed on funny. And George's family's been a question mark for decades. Doesn't mean a thing in the end. George and Darlene aren't descended from that particular daughter. Her name was Elspeth. She had a daughter herself, but I never heard any mention of insan…ity." He clutched his seat as a furious gust of wind buffeted the car. "Felt like a giant tried to grab us and missed."

Isabella avoided a pothole the size of a moon crater, then leaned forward to peer through the windshield. "The gate's open, and I see Donovan's truck. I wish I knew if that was good."

"Won't know till we get inside, will we?"

She could tell by the way he squared up that inside Darkwood Manor was the last place Haden wanted to go. She didn't blame him. With thunder making the ground beneath them tremble and lightning splitting an ominous black sky, it was a daunting prospect.

The key was to stay calm and focused. Donovan wouldn't be taken in easily, and in any case, Darlene thought her partner was afraid of him—at least he was in his Dr. Jekyll mode. As Mr. Hyde, Isabella suspected he might be much bolder.

Oh, great, she reflected in exasperation. Now the nerves that had been zinging inside her since she and Haden left town were really going off. Shoving them back in line, she pushed the front door open and ventured into the gloom.

It was a bit like stepping over some nether-dimensional threshold and into the Twilight Zone. Haden's fists bunched around the back of her coat. An icy draft blew across her cheeks. Rain pummeled the ancient roof. The wind moaned through cracks high in the rafters.

"He's here," Haden croaked in her ear. "I can feel him. He's watching everything we do."

With her heart beating in her throat, Isabella shone her flashlight around the cobwebbed entry hall. "I don't know if I want you to be talking about Darlene's partner or Aaron Dark's ghost."

"One's no different than the other in my book."

Reaching sideways, she groped for the wall switch. "Donovan?"

Of course he didn't answer, but to her overwhelming relief, when she tried it, the feeble overhead light flickered on.

"Oh, well now, that's better." Haden loosened his stranglehold long enough to swipe a hand across his forehead. "Thought for a minute my heart was going to punch its way out of my chest." Massaging his ribs, he handed her the abused family tree, gave her cell phone a shake and tried Donovan's number again. He had his thumb on the redial button when a low moan emerged from the ballroom.

Isabella's eyes whipped to the doorway. Her mouth went dry. "That wasn't the wind," she whispered.

Haden gave his head a terrified shake.

A sudden, horrifying thought struck, and with Donovan's name frozen on her lips, she took off across the littered floor.

She saw him in her mind, but couldn't, wouldn't, let the image solidify. A trained federal agent would not allow himself to be blindsided by a fool.

When Haden endeavored to catch her, she knocked his hand away and slapped on the overhead light. In the weak glow at the far end of the room, she was just able to make out a shape. Not a crumpled tarp like the first day, but a man in black, lying in a heap on the floor.

Haden finally pinned her arms and held on. "You said there were traps in here. Big ones."

"I know." She pried on his fingers. "I'll watch for them."

"But," he began, then heaved out a breath. "Aw, hell, let's go, then. But carefully. This could be a trick."

Outside, the wind howled. Something large hit the wall. A tree limb scratched at the window.

The lone lightbulb swayed at the end of a long, frayed cord. The man on the floor moaned again and stirred.

Isabella walked cautiously toward him. Every pulse in her body jumped. Her fist closed on the paper in her hand. Haden had a chokehold on her coat.

The thirty seconds it took them to work their way across the floor felt like thirty minutes.

"Stop, stop," Haden whispered. "I saw something move near the wall."

"There's a cat here." Isabella kept her eyes on the now motionless man. Was that blood seeping onto the debris around his body?

She crept closer, circled until the side of his face came into view. When it did, she gasped softly and dropped to her knees. Setting the paper down, she crawled forward, touched his neck.

Haden crawled behind her. "Is he alive?"

"I think so." She struggled to think past the scream in her head. "Barely, though. Call 911." Leaning closer, she said, "Don't move, okay? We're getting help."

One eye opened to stare at her. An outstretched finger crooked.

"Don't move," she said again, but didn't think he heard her. Was sure of it a moment later when he coughed and blood dribbled from his mouth.

The staring eye took on a glassy sheen. The bent finger stopped moving.

She touched his neck again, then released a shaky breath, and sat back on her heels.

"He's gone," she said dully. She knew Haden didn't hear her. He was shouting at the 911 operator and gesturing wildly at Ridge Road.

"It's Darlene's partner," he yelled into the phone. "She

thought he might try to hurt Isabella, but it looks like he's hurt himself."

Reaching over, Isabella pried the cell phone from his hand. "It's too late," she told the woman. The scream in her head slithered downward. "He's dead. Gunshot or stab wound, I can't be sure. Yes, I know him." She couldn't drag her gaze from the single, lifeless eye, had to force the words past the lump in her throat. "He lives in Mystic Harbor. He's a Realtor. He goes by the name Gordie Tallahassee."

Chapter Sixteen

"We can't stay here." Haden's fingers were cutting off the circulation in Isabella's arm. "We can't leave." His head swiveled every which way. "We have to do something."

"I know." But all she could think about right then was Donovan. "He gave me a gun," she recalled as they backtracked to the entry hall. "It's in my car."

"We can lock ourselves inside, wait for the paramedics."

Or the deputies, Isabella thought. One of them, an older man, was slow but efficient. He might be willing to help them find Donovan. As for Orry...

The lights around them, already dim, began to flicker and fade. They retreated into the storm and finally reached her car. Isabella scrabbled through the glove box until she found Donovan's backup gun.

"Should we go and meet whoever's first on the road?" Haden sounded frantic. He rubbed his palms on the legs of his pants. "Don't wanna leave Donovan, but he's had a lot of training, and we haven't. What do you think?"

The sound of cracking wood prevented Isabella from answering. Grabbing Haden's arm, she stared in fascinated horror as a large tree started to list.

"Out, out, out," Haden yelled, and plunged from his seat to the puddled ground.

Isabella did the same, then scrambled to her feet and ran.

Behind them, the tree gave a drunken lurch. When the wind swooped down again, the trunk broke in two.

The base didn't hit her car, but the outermost branches hit on the roof as the behemoth pine landed, bounced and eventually settled.

"Back inside," she shouted to Haden, who gaped at the destruction. She tugged on his arm. "We can't stay out here."

Huge gusts of wind buffeted them. Even Haden with his bulk made little headway against it. Planting both hands on her back, he shoved until they were inside, panting and rattled and no safer in Isabella's opinion then if they'd been standing under the felled pine.

The racket of the storm diminished once they wrestled the door closed. Isabella pushed wet strands of hair from her face and ordered herself to think. Donovan was here somewhere. So were a dead man and a murderer.

Gordie Tallahassee had been Darlene's partner, one she'd come to view as dangerous. So who'd killed him, and why? And where was Donovan?

Pressing her fingers to her temples, she lowered herself onto a broad tread at the base of the staircase.

Haden sat with her for a moment, then pulled a large handkerchief from his jacket pocket and stood to pace. The Dark family tree he'd stuffed in with it landed on the stairs next to her hip.

Overhead, the light shivered and danced. Isabella lowered her hands and adjusted her grip on Donovan's gun.

Orry had come here with him today. Not willingly, but he'd come. Was that a good or bad thing? Was there more to the acting sheriff than anyone knew?

She didn't realize she was staring at the light until her vision began to go spotty.

"Stop it," she said out loud and wrenched her gaze from the trembling bulb. "Donovan's fine. He'll be fine. Maybe he's already caught the person who killed Gordie."

More big branches thudded against the roof and walls. Thunder crashed directly over the peak.

The scream in Isabella's head returned. She closed her eyes, fought it. Opened them, breathed in, then out. Skimmed over a name on the paper beside her and looked away.

Lightning shot through the blackened sky. With it, as if jolted from some dusty corner of her mind, a memory shimmered to life.

"Morris." She repeated the surname she'd just glimpsed. Wanted to shake it off, but couldn't. Picking up the family tree, she read the name again and felt her blood turn to ice water.

The lines of descent went up, down and sideways. To the left, she saw the name Georgina—George—Solomon Calvert. To the right, in a line that came down from Aaron and on through his niece Elspeth, a woman called Davina Morris.

"Oh—my—God!" A thud reached her as she stood in slow motion, paper in hand. "Haden, I know one of the people on this tree. Davina Morris was married for eighteen months. She and her husband had a son called Da—" Her eyes came up. The name stuck briefly then slipped out in a shocked whisper "—vid."

"HELLO, ISABELLA." A grin of delight stretched her ex-boyfriend's mouth like a rubber band. It widened the longer she stared. But what else could she do? She was having a nightmare. No, worse, a night terror.

David Morris Gimbel was dead. She'd seen the death

certificate. She'd gone to the funeral, to the reading of his will. She'd put flowers on his grave.

A thousand thoughts raced through her head.

He'd knocked Haden out. That was the thump she'd heard a moment ago. He'd undoubtedly murdered Gordie Tallahassee as well.

What else might he have done?

Keeping her eyes on his face, she raised her gun to his chest. "Where's Donovan?" she demanded and watched humor descend into disappointment.

"Is that all you have to say? I return from the dead—oh, the miracle of it—and you ask me about a man who's as good as dead himself?"

She understood enough about the situation and David not to let him see the relief that swamped her. "You're a Dark," she stated without inflection. "That's why you bought the manor."

He wagged a finger. "No, no, no, that's how I was able to fast-talk the coot who owned it into selling me the manor. Oh, I laid it on thick, Isabella. I believe at one point I actually welled up. As for the actual purchase, I did that for an entirely different reason."

She could see Haden breathing, but again let nothing show. Wasn't sure what to show in any case. Fear might excite David. Anger might send him right over the slippery edge.

When he made a move toward her, she straight-armed the gun.

The smile returned to his lips. "Sweet Isabella…" Tutting, he extended his hands, palms up. "You wouldn't shoot an unarmed man."

"Where's Donovan, David? Where's Katie? Why the elaborate charade?"

"All good questions. Lower the gun, and I'll give you some good answers."

"Move away from Haden first."

He set a hand over his heart. "I'm wounded, truly wounded. You think I'd kick a man when he's down? Or no, wait." Altering the position of his upturned palms, he twirled in a slow circle. "You must be thinking I'd—" he whipped out a nine-millimeter Glock, aimed it at Haden's head "—kill him."

David's dark eyes glittered with an intensity that sent needles of fear through every part of Isabella's body.

"Since I'm the one who toppled him, you'd be right about that. Drop the gun, Bella, or Uncle Bear becomes part of the dust he's laying in."

He'd do it, she realized, in a heartbeat. Absorbing his fierce stare, she lowered her arms.

"Pretty sure I said drop it, sweetheart."

She glanced at Haden and complied.

A lopsided grin crooked David's mouth. "She always was a smart cookie," he said with a wink for the unconscious man at his feet. "That's why I chose her to be my forever paramour. I'd say wife, but the connotations aren't as glamorous, are they, or as intriguing? That was Aaron's mistake. He married Sybil and in so doing took the edge off their romance. She was forced to seek her titillation elsewhere. Like Isabella did when she thought I was dead." His eyes hardened to stone. "You can imagine how peeved I was to discover that she had feelings for your soon-to-be departed nephew. But of course those feelings were false." He half squeezed the trigger of his gun, smiled with his teeth only. "Weren't they, darling?"

"Yes," she said quickly. "Completely false. Donovan's not… He means nothing to me."

The smile spread, but still didn't touch his eyes. "Did I

say smart cookie? I meant brilliant cookie. Tell me you love me, Bella."

She struggled to keep her fingers from balling into fists. "Tell me where Katie is first. And Don—Haden's nephew."

"Brilliant," David repeated and gave Haden's leg a none-too-gentle kick. "Oops, said I wouldn't do that, didn't I?"

"Please, David, where are they?"

He set a sneakered foot on the big man's back, released a gusty breath. "So stubborn... Whoa!" He glanced at the trembling ceiling. "That was some peal of thunder. Think my gun might make a bigger boom?"

Before she could respond, he snapped the barrel sideways and blasted out one of the windows.

"Oh, damn, now this beautiful entryway's going to get all wet. We'll have to relocate, Bella. Question is..." Crouching, he stuck the smoking barrel into Haden's temple. "Do we leave Uncle Bear alive, or as dead as the brainless moron in the other room?" He cupped a palm to his ear. "I believe I hear the sound of approaching sirens. Your choice, my darling. You've got five seconds." He put visible pressure on the trigger. "Now you've got four...three...two..."

DISCOVERING THAT SOMEONE wanted him dead came as no surprise to Donovan. It wasn't the first time, and it wasn't important. Only Isabella's safety mattered.

"I swear," the man he was holding insisted, "I didn't get a good look at the guy. Only people I bother to notice are women."

Donovan regarded him for a long moment, decided he was probably telling the truth and released him with a shove. "Go on, beat it. Don't let me see you again."

The man, who claimed his name was Smith, started off. After ten yards, however, he turned back. "The lady you're worried about took the heat off me for a while. She's pretty and my cat liked her, so I'll tell you this before I disappear. The guy who wants you dead left something hanging outside the ballroom the day before your girlfriend got caught in that foot trap. I took it because I thought the stone in the center might be a diamond." He fished in a grubby pocket. "You can decide if it helps."

He handed Donovan a key ring with a heavy silver fob, an empty spot where a gemstone might have been mounted, and three carved initials.

DMG.

IF HE'D HAD A MOMENT to spare, it might have surprised Donovan that Orry kept pace with him in the tunnels. As it was, all he could think about was Isabella and the danger she'd be in if DMG—David Morris Gimbel—got hold of her.

"I don't understand," Orry panted in his wake. "You say Gimbel's after her, but he's dead. I was at the accident site with Sheriff Crookshank. Car was there, body was there and your own uncle was talking to him when he flew over the cliff. The first mate on Milt Walker's fishing boat saw a red Corvette go up in flames."

"The car crashed and burned, Orry, and someone's body with it. But it wasn't David Gimbel's."

"That's crazy. Are you sure this Smith character wasn't just spinning a convenient yarn?"

"I'd say the odds are in his favor." He just hoped like hell they were in Isabella's as well.

"So Gimbel's alive and…what? I assume there's a point to everything he's done. I mean, other than he's a loon and needs a long rest in a rubber room. Why the elaborate charade?"

It was a question Donovan had been asking himself for several hundred yards now, with no satisfactory answers.

Gimbel obviously had an agenda, one that was unlikely to involve the local twosome Smith had also spotted slinking around the manor, planting ankle traps and ball bearings and arrows in front doors.

Orry's breathing became a wheeze, but that didn't stop him from puffing out another question. "Why did he—shoot at us—on the cliff?"

Donovan veered left at the fork. "I don't think he did. I'll explain that part of it later. Right now, we need to get back into the manor."

"Ho, wait, what?" Orry grabbed his arm and dragged him to a halt. "In case you've forgotten, there's a nutcase wandering around that house. Call me a bad sport, but I'd rather not wind up on a slab in the town morgue."

Bending at the waist, Donovan took a precious moment to breathe. "Gimbel didn't set those traps in the ballroom, Orry. He didn't shoot at us, and he isn't responsible for that wail we've been hearing."

"But…"

"I don't have time for this, okay? I have to trust the caveman, and you have to trust me. Gimbel wants Isabella. I'm guessing alive, but I have no idea why or how long he intends to keep her that way. What I do know is that I'm going to stop him. Now, you can either come along and help, or get yourself out of here. One way or another, I'm going up. Savvy?"

The deputy stared and finally nodded. "Yeah, okay, I'm in. I'll—" Exhausted, he motioned forward. "Go."

It took them an eternity, and a number of wrong turns to backtrack to the ballroom entrance. The hidden door, Donovan noticed, was closed. Exchanging gun for light, he angled his beam upward.

Orry opted not to wait. He brushed past and mounted the stone stairs. He was banging on the stuck frame when Donovan spied the trip wire. Swearing, he took the stairs two at a time. "Orry, don't! There's a—"

It was all he got out. A second later, the wire snapped, the door exploded and both the deputy and Donovan were flung to the rocky ground below.

SOMETHING—NOT THUNDER—blasted through the passage-way with enough force to make the battery lamps David had wedged into the stone walls quiver.

Steps in front of him, Isabella spun. She saw the bottled amusement on his face and fought to contain her panic. "What have you done?"

"With any luck, Bella, dear, I've annihilated the competition."

An iron band tightened around her lungs. He nodded enthusiastically at the horror she couldn't mask.

"Yes, that's it. Kaboom. Bye-bye fed. Of course, I'll have to make sure he's dead, but it's an excellent bet. I prob-ably should have offed his Bigfoot uncle, too. You like him, though, and he didn't see me, and I wanted to throw you a bone since I'll have to do something rather dastardly before I'm done here."

Isabella's mind reeled, but she held fast to her conviction. David Gimbel wasn't clever enough to kill Donovan.

Because she knew he wanted her to react, she turned and continued walking. "You're despicable, David. But you needn't have gone to such extremes. I told you, I wasn't in love with Donovan."

"Uh-huh. Well, I'd say I wasted a perfectly good bomb, but the thing is, no matter how you felt about him, the late Agent Black was in love with you."

"What is it you want from me?"

"Nothing *from* you, darling." He enunciated the words. "I simply want you. Your affection would be nice, but your physical presence will do if that's all you've got to give."

"Is that supposed to be an answer?"

"It's a very precise answer." Zipping up close behind her, he used his gun to play with her hair. "You see, my pretty, you left me. Decided I wasn't the man for you and walked away. Just like Sybil walked away from Aaron."

"Sybil had a lover. And she didn't walk, she ran."

"Minor difference. One day she belonged to Aaron, the next she didn't, or claimed she didn't. So he hunted her down, killed her lover and imprisoned her. We'll set aside the fact that she was pregnant with lover boy's child, because I'm certain it doesn't apply insofar as our parallel story is concerned. The point is, he meant to keep her locked up for life, and that's precisely the plan I have for you." His tone took on a mirthful edge. "Too bad about the dastardly part."

Isabella wondered how she managed to stay on her feet when her legs had turned to rubber. Somehow she cast him an unperturbed look. "There's worse you can do than plot a lifelong abduction and commit multiple acts of murder?"

He rocked his head back and forth. "Maybe not in the grand scheme. But on a personal level—aren't you forgetting someone?"

"I told you, David, I didn't love…" She caught back a sudden breath. "Katie!"

The gun stroked her cheek. "Interesting that your cousin seems to have slipped to the perimeter of your mind. I mean, with you two being so close and all, and Donovan meaning less than nothing to you."

Isabella's temper sparked to life. "Must be the shock of seeing you again. And maybe having your gun in my face."

"Oh, come now, Bella, you can't really expect me to trust you. I might be a Dark by birth, but I'm also an attorney with a cynical side to my personality. By the way, do you still like squab?"

"I never liked squab."

His jaw dropped. "You mean you lied?"

Too late, she spied the trap. "I was being polite," she told him. "I didn't want to hurt your sister's feelings."

"Stepsister. One you referred to more than once as Cruella DeVillain." He jabbed the underside of her chin with his Glock. "You love him, don't you?"

She strove for a calm tone. "Does it matter?"

"I'll let you know. Go on, keep walking. We're almost there." Before she could, however, he set his mouth next to her ear, blew lightly at her hair. When he didn't draw the expected shiver, he sighed. "So stubborn." He gave her a shove. "Okay, move. I've hung around this town too long as it is. Planted an earring for you. That was finally discovered. Left a rather distinctive calling card with my initials on it as well. Unfortunately, someone got there before you and stole it. You just can't trust anyone these days, can you, babe? And we both know how our outing in the van went thanks to your dead fed." He blew in her ear, then gave her another shove. "Stop dragging your feet, Isabella. Revised or not, I've got a schedule to keep."

"A sched—" She stopped the question when he giggled. *Giggled?*

He crawled his fingers up and over her shoulder. "You want to punch me, don't you, Bella? You're hoping, praying that the fed's not dead, and the Dark knight will rush in to thwart the Dark prince." His voice softened to an eerie whisper. "Don't hold your breath, sweetheart. I used a heavy hand when wiring my explosive device." He hooked his gun arm around Isabella's neck. "You're it for getting yourself out of here." Keeping his voice genial, he gave her throat a squeeze. "Meantime, would you care to hear my plan?"

"Do I have a choice?"

A chuckle emerged. "Stubborn." He kissed her temple, forced her to walk. "I've got two actually. The preferred plan and the alternate. In the preferred version, you and I fly to a lovely Caribbean island I purchased last summer under a false name. We live there together in total seclusion. Supply ships come at regular intervals. We're happy, Bella, truly happy and very much alive."

"David…"

"Shh." He gave her lips a light tap with his index finger. "I'm not finished. In the alternate version, you refuse to come around, because, face it, you're James Corrigan's granddaughter. Still, what's mine remains mine."

The pressure around her throat increased dramatically. "David, you're choking me."

His face lit up. "Exactly. Nail on the head." He nuzzled her ear. "Unpreferred scenario? If you refuse to cooperate, or you try to trick me, I lock you in a tropical tower." Another giggle emerged. "And then I kill you."

Chapter Seventeen

He got rough after that, kissing her with a savagery that had panic sprinting through every nerve in her body.

When he finished abusing her mouth, he sank his hand into her hair and dragged her down a poorly lit passage to a cul-de-sac set high enough in the cliff that the tidewater couldn't reach it. He'd fastened a pair of tubular battery lamps to the stone wall. They illuminated the area, revealing a cot in one corner, a three-legged stool beside it and a stash of supplies in open crates in the shadow.

"All the comforts of home, baby." Giving her hair a twist, he tossed her in. "Food, seating, bed. Wanna try the last one out?"

His eyes looked feral. His lip glistened with sweat. Isabella rubbed the back of her head and wisely held her tongue.

He walked back and forth in the opening, pushed his hands through his hair until it stood up in tufts. "You left me," he said at length. "You told me we weren't right for each other, then you flew off to Bangkok."

She watched his face. "You agreed we should end it."

He stopped pacing to stare. "Excuse me, but were we in the same room when this happened? Because in my memory, you did all the talking. You admitted you were selfish and self-centered, and that I was far too good for you—which of course I am. But who were you to be telling me it was over between us?"

"David, I didn't say any of those…" At a vicious look from him, she stopped. "Never mind."

"It was all about you, that night and every other. What you wanted, how you thought our life should be, how lonely you were living in this isolated place, how you deserved to be happy even if I couldn't understand why you weren't already."

Was there any point arguing? Isabella wondered. His fantasy appeared firmly entrenched.

He stabbed an accusing finger at her. "I decide the whens and ifs of things, Bella, no one else. Not you, not my legal partner, not the Cinderella stepsiblings I've been forced to endure since my mother ditched my father and remarried without a second thought for how I might feel. 'Come and get us, Daddy,' I used to pray. Grow some balls and snatch her back. Get me the hell away from these people. But he never did. Mama Davina got what Sybil wanted, and I got punished. Thank you, Sybil Dark."

He all but spat the name, and Isabella didn't know whether to sympathize, rationalize or say nothing until he ran down. She opted for the third thing and kept a close eye on his gun hand.

"I've often dreamed about killing my mother. Who knows, maybe one day I will. Right now, though, I'll settle for satisfying my own desires and showing Aaron how it could have been for him if he'd handled things better." He looked left, then right, then bent forward to stage-whisper, "The man had no finesse. Not his fault, really—he lived in an archaic time." Another stage whisper, this one punctuated by a tinkling laugh. "No birth control."

"David, don't you think—?"

"Shut up," he warned, raising his gun. Then he smiled

and extended his hands in a show of pride. "Once again, she does as she's told. Brilliant and obedient. I am the luckiest of men."

Isabella forced herself to think past what he'd said, what he'd done, what he planned to do. He'd kill her without hesitation; he'd made that clear. He didn't love her—also clear—he simply couldn't accept that she'd ended their so-called relationship.

He continued to walk back and forth. With each passing minute, his stride grew shorter, his body language more agitated.

Afraid to move, Isabella waited him out. Adopt the wrong expression, he might snap. Say the wrong thing, he might shoot her.

He began to mutter and tick items off on his fingers. "Whack a homeless guy, stuff him in the Corvette. Hated to see that go. Lucky, timely phone call. Cliff coming. Jump. Bye-bye, homeless guy. Burn well in my stead. Fast-forward now. Swiss bank account. Money out, money in. Shuffle it around. Too bad about cousin Burt and that big old bottle of wine someone—me—gave him. Guy was eighty-two, lived in Smallville, Louisiana." He snorted out a laugh. "Like anyone there would have thought to check the briefly rich and suddenly deceased recluse for signs of poison. Inheritance takes roundabout route back to source. All tracks and bases covered. We're cool." Straightening, he turned to beam at Isabella. "Only one thing left to do, my dear. Well, two, but I won't make you look at messy body parts, even if I still think you loved him. You know what the first thing is, don't you? Come on, be clever. Dastardly," he reminded her when she didn't respond.

Her heart thumped. "Oh, God, David, don't hurt Katie."

Mortified, he drew back. "You think I'd hurt your favorite

cousin? I'd have to be a monster to do that." Cocking his gun, he took one-eyed aim at Isabella's throat. "Quick and painless is the way. One shot. I promise, my darling, she won't feel a—" his brow furrowed "—thing." He spun so fast, Isabella missed the move. "What was that?" he demanded. "I heard a sound."

She glanced at the light on her left, took a careful step toward it. "I didn't hear anything."

"There was a squish."

"Maybe it was a rat."

"Rats don't wear shoes." Baring his teeth, he fired into the shadows. Bits of rock scattered in all directions.

Because she knew it was the only opportunity she'd get, Isabella grabbed the battery light from the wall beside her and smashed it against the stones. She had the second one in her grasp when he swung back and planted a bullet mere inches above her head.

She waited until he whirled, then snatched up the second light and slammed it onto the floor.

"Stop doing that!" He started spinning in circles. "This is my plan! You're my woman! These are my tunnels!"

With the shadows much denser now, she ducked into the supply area in the corner, scrambled to find anything that might work as a weapon.

The best she could manage was a tall bottle that felt like wine.

"Stop, stop, stop!" David screamed.

More bullets and rock fragments flew. Something—a cat?—hissed. His scream became a startled curse. Seconds later, a hand clamped itself over Isabella's mouth, and a voice she didn't recognize growled at her to start crawling.

Although she didn't argue, she had no idea where she was going or who was pushing on her butt.

"You're dead!" David shrieked. "Do you hear me, Bella?"

A bullet whizzed past her cheek.

The man behind her pushed harder. "All this for a bunch of frigging antiques. Get the lead out, lady."

She glimpsed snatches of motion ahead of them. An arm, a sneaker, then finally, a streak of black leather...

"Donovan!" Relief made her muscles go weak. "I knew he wasn't dead."

"We will be if you don't stop dawdling," the man behind her growled.

"I'm not dawdling. You're shoving me into a wall."

"Go the other way then, and let's get—*oomph*."

With a loud expulsion of air, his body knocked her into the wall. Before she could turn, a pair of hands came down on her throat.

"No—one—takes—what's—mine!" David ground out.

Terror spiked, but only for a moment. Then his hands were gone, and she fell back into the stones.

Something skittered across the ground.

"Got you now, lover boy," David crowed. "I'll tell Sybil you went down swinging."

Dazed, Isabella pushed herself upright, shook her head. Her eyes had adjusted enough that she could see David taking aim in silhouette. She shouted his name.

A single bullet rang out. Wheeling to face her, David smirked. Then the smirk faded, and he dropped his arms. After wobbling for a moment, he pitched forward to land less than a foot in front of her.

Leaving the man who'd been shoving her to mutter in the deep shadows, Isabella scanned the area ahead until she found Donovan. He was bruised and bloody and down on one knee. The black cat sat beside him. A dying battery lamp flickered behind him. She saw the faintest of smiles cross his lips. Then his own arm dropped, the light went out, and everything around them went dark.

"I CAN'T TAKE IT ANYMORE," Haden declared. "All these dreadful shenanigans going on in our quiet little town. I've a mind to pack up and move to Nova Scotia." He flapped a big hand, but otherwise didn't rouse himself from the dramatic sprawl he'd adopted in the waiting room of Mystic Harbor Hospital. "Any word on Donovan yet?"

"No." And the worry of that had Isabella prowling the waiting room like a caged tiger.

Wincing, Haden poked at his head. "Don't you fret about him. Boy's got a thick skull. A few bumps and bruises won't faze him. Now, Orry's in a lot sorrier state, or so he'll insist. Not because he really is, but as a way to keep public—and he'll be hoping his wife's—sympathy on his side." A dark eye cracked open to glare at Darlene, who was slumped on the couch across from him. "Way I see it, you're the one needs her head examined. Having sex with Orry? Dammit, girl, you went to school with him and his wife. You ought to be ashamed."

Arms folded, George stared her sulky daughter down. "An affair with Orry's the tip of the iceberg, Haden. My girl here was in cahoots with Gordie. She was trying to frighten Isabella into selling the manor and leaving town. All so she could get out herself."

A defiant Darlene fixed her gaze on the floor. "I wrote her a note, warning her off when I thought Gordie was getting too weird." Her eyes flicked to Isabella. "I used a sample of poppy red lipstick."

"After you pretended to be Aaron Dark's ghost, set up an old suit in one of the manor windows and took three shots at both your lover and your cousin." George tapped a foot. "Honestly, Darlene, if you didn't look so miserable, I'd take you over my knee and wallop you. But sheriff Crookshank'll be bringing enough charges against you that a wallop will seem tame by comparison. And don't you go giving me any pitiful looks. You did the deeds, you can just pay the price. Wailings and warnings, arrows in doors, a rattlesnake in bed…"

"The rattlesnake was Gordie's doing. I didn't know anything about it. Yes to the wail and the warnings, but not the snake."

"Orry wasn't involved?"

"No."

"If that's true, why did he spend so much time skulking around the manor?" Isabella asked. "And don't say he was looking for Katie."

Darlene shrugged. "He was probably looking for me. I think he thought I was sleeping with someone other than him."

"Oh, for heaven's sake." Throwing up her hands, George spun away. "Yell at her, will you, Isabella?"

"I'm too worried about Donovan and Katie to yell." She sent Darlene a pleasant smile. "I'll take a rain check, though."

George patted her shoulder. "Donovan'll be fine. Haden's right—we Dark descendants have heads of stone. But how's your poor cousin doing? She must have been terrified tied up in that horrible underground little niche."

Isabella tried not to recall the expression on Katie's face when she and Donovan, who'd refused to leave the tunnels until they located her, had followed David's trail of battery lamps to another cul-de-sac close to the one where he'd trapped Isabella.

She'd been bound and gagged for days. Fed, but also threatened every time one of David's attempts to abduct Isabella had failed.

"I don't know why he kept me alive, Bella," she'd confided on the way back to the house. "Maybe he thought he could use me to draw you in. I should have screamed when I spotted him at the manor, but I was just so shocked. I turned around, and there he was, big as life and twice as crazy. I don't like to wish people dead, but his death was probably a blessing for everyone involved, including him."

When a voice came over the hospital PA system, Isabella refocused on her surroundings.

George returned to the couch to harangue Darlene. Haden continued to probe his bandaged head. Out in the hall, Orry's wife marched back and forth, tight-lipped and scowling.

Isabella murmured, "Would not want to be you right now, Acting Sheriff. Haden, are you sure you shouldn't spend the night here?"

His horrified expression said it all.

Slipping past the angry Ms. Lucas, Isabelle walked to the far end of the corridor. Voices rose and fell above background music that managed to sound equal parts soothing and eerie.

Outside, the storm still vented its rage on the town. Through the top of the window, she saw lightning bolts snake down in the vicinity of Darkwood Manor.

"Looks like Aaron's in a bad mood."

"Donovan!" She turned to face him so quickly they almost banged heads. "You're—wow—" She drew back in shock. "You're all black and blue." Half afraid to touch, she set a gentle fingertip on his bruised cheekbone. "Are you sure you shouldn't be in bed?"

"That bad, huh?"

"Worse than bad." Her eyes slid to the graze on his temple. "Do I want to know what the rest of you looks like?"

"Picture a half-wrapped mummy. My right shoulder took the biggest hit. Not from the explosion, but from Orry falling on me."

She trailed that same gentle finger under his lower lip. "No damage to your mouth, I see. That part's good."

He offered a faint smile. "You want to punch me, don't you?"

Amusement kindled. "Only because I was terrified when I saw you almost collapse in the tunnel. I knew you'd been careless because of me." Since he was obviously able to walk upright, she nudged him with her hip. "That's at least ten years off my life, Black. Not as a result of what David did, but from seeing you after he was dead. Dead again." She exhaled her frustration. "Whatever he is or was, I'm just glad the nightmare's over."

With the admission came an overwhelming and unanticipated sense of exhaustion. The moment Donovan eased her head onto his shoulder, the room began to fade in and out.

"I wouldn't let myself believe he'd killed you. Didn't matter how clever he claimed to have been, I knew you were alive." She breathed in the scent of leather and rain and soap and man, waited for the tremor of residual fear to pass, then raised her head. "Who was that man in the tunnel, by the way? The one who grabbed me and shoved me into a wall while you and David were going at each other?"

"He says his name's Smith. It's not, but it doesn't matter. My guess is he's a smuggler, and he's been using the caves under Dark Ridge as an offload point for his merchandise."

"Stolen?"

"Probably. I made a call to a friend in Portland."

"But he—Smith—helped you tonight. Helped me, anyway. Is it right to turn him in?"

"I gave him twenty-four hours, Isabella. He'll contact his partner. They'll close down local operations."

"Is that what you call an exchange of favors?"

"In a sense. I think we'll discover the goods he's been smuggling have already been stolen by someone else."

"So he's robbing from the rich thieves to give to the poor ones. Why did he agree to help you, and is the cat I saw okay?"

"Cat's fine. It's his. And he helped me because the way the tunnels twist and turn placed us at the same hidden entrance at the same time. The door blew, I fell on Smith, Orry fell on me. The cat watched the whole thing from a safe distance."

She dropped her cheek back onto his shoulder. "Whatever his deal is, I owe him for finding Katie's watch, then giving it away. It added weight to a story Orry would have otherwise dismissed. Speaking of—how is the acting sheriff?"

"Alive." Donovan glanced at the woman now whipping to and fro with balled fists and a very flushed face. "For the moment."

"Bless me!" Haden exclaimed behind them. "You look like you've been to hell and back two or three times!"

Lumbering out of the shadows, he hauled the pair of them into a huge bear hug. Then he clapped massive hands onto his nephew's shoulders, winked at Isabella and announced to everyone within earshot—pretty much the entire ground floor—that there would be a big celebration at his restaurant tomorrow night. Drinks and food would be free, and no one, not even Darlene, would be turned away.

"As for you, Isabella." He gave her a series of small pats on her back. "You look all in."

"Feel it," she agreed. "Is Katie…asleep…?"

If Haden answered, she didn't hear him. The shadows were creating weird patterns in her head. She knew it was Donovan who lifted her into his arms, and she wanted to object, but the shadows refused to abate.

In her hazing mind, she watched Aaron Dark's eyes

transform into David's then slowly into Donovan's. And for the first time since coming to Mystic Harbor, tumbled into a deep, dreamless sleep.

Epilogue

It didn't end with anything as simple as a good night's rest.
There were still questions to be asked and answered, deaths
to be accounted for and apologies to be made.

With Orry adamantly out of commission, the older, pokier
deputy took over. Left to him, Isabella figured matters might
be sorted out by June. Fortunately for everyone involved,
Sheriff Crookshank planned to return in a few days.

Katie recovered to tell her story. She explained that after
David took her, he used her cell phone to contact Isabella,
presumably in an attempt to prevent any unwanted investigation into her disappearance. As he'd readily admitted, it was
David who'd abducted Isabella in the van and also David
she'd run into the day she'd followed Smuggler Smith's cat
into the corridor at Darkwood.

Pouting and with her arms tightly crossed, Darlene approached her to insist she hadn't known about David or his
plan. She'd assumed Gordie was behind all the nastiness.

People came and went from the sheriff's office for most
of the day. When darkness descended, however, so did
Haden—like a drill sergeant. He told Donovan to handle
the bar and asked Isabella to take the drink orders. Then
he dusted off his hands and gave a firm nod. "Let's see you
two avoid each other now."

Isabella could have told him she hadn't been avoiding

Donovan all day, but why bother? He'd been avoiding her, so it was much the same thing in the end.

Not every resident of Mystic Harbor crowded into the Cave that night, but a good three-quarters of them did, and they all wanted to hear the gory details. Another Dark gone mad, and how intriguing that this one bore a real-life resemblance to his ancestor, Aaron. The Historical Society was in seventh heaven.

Isabella answered more questions in three hours than she usually did in three months. Katie was offered a wicked deal on a used car—still no idea where her old one had gone—from a man who wanted not only her business, but also her company for the remainder of the evening.

"No need to look so concerned, hon," a tipsy George assured her. "That's my cousin once removed Katie's canoodling with. He's a sweet young man under the blather. And while we're on the subject…" She motioned toward the bar. "Donovan's looking a tad lonely back there."

"I think he likes it that way."

"Bluster, pure bluster. Go on over," she urged. "Have it out with him. My money's on you to bash down that all-Darks-are-cut-from-the-same-mold barrier before the night's done."

"Your faith is staggering."

"So's my daughter's gall, and thank you again for not pressing charges. She's just damn lucky she didn't wind up like Gordie, though it's hard to say what state she'll be in if Orry's wife gets hold of her."

Isabella grinned at the mental picture. "Similar state to Orry, I imagine." She hugged the older woman. "Thanks for the boot in the butt."

"Anytime."

Handing her tray to Lindsay, Isabella pushed up her sleeves and zeroed in on the bartender.

Donovan was drawing a mug of beer when she planted her hands on the counter and said straight-out, "We can we talk here or take it outside, Black. Your choice."

Lips curving, he topped the mug and slid it the length of the bar to a harassed-looking Robert Drake.

Isabella did a surprised double take. "He's still here?"

"He wasn't involved," Donovan reminded her.

"What about that message he gave George asking me to meet you at the manor?"

"The call was real, Isabella. It was placed from a phone booth near the harbor. Darlene says Gordie wanted you to experience the wail at close range."

"The wail and Darlene's ghostly warning for me to run." She regarded the developer in some amusement. "Looks like he's made a conquest. That's Orry's wife who's draped all over him, isn't it?"

"Ever since he came in." Trapping her chin, Donovan drew her across the bar. "You said outside, right?"

As always, when faced with those mesmerizing eyes, she could do little more than nod.

Thick fog had rolled in on the heels of last night's storm. Layers of mist slunk around the back door and crawled along the old brick walls.

Buttoning her coat, Isabella stepped into the alley. A gasp stuttered out when Donovan caught her arm and twirled her around.

His mouth was on hers before she could react. Ten hot, hungry seconds later, she had a spinning head, a jumble of displaced thoughts and a tingling sensation on her lips that lingered long after he stepped away.

It took several seconds for her head to clear. "That was— amazing. Is there a reason you look like you want to hit someone?"

"I don't want to care about you, Isabella."

"I gathered that." Fascinated, she touched her lips. Still tingling.

"David Gimbel was insane."

"Yes, that one was even harder to miss."

"He left the bulk of his estate to a very old, very distant relative."

"Cousin Burt. David poisoned him."

Donovan shot her an unreadable look. "At which point, having conned the old guy into signing a will he'd drafted beforehand, he proceeded to funnel the money into a Swiss bank account."

"I got the gist of the story in the tunnels. David's plan was to take me to a Caribbean island he owned and keep me there forever. Dead or alive, it didn't matter which. I belonged to him, and no one was allowed to take what was his. I have to tell you, the whole thing makes me feel icky in retrospect."

"Why icky?"

"Let me think. Maybe because I dated him for two months and never saw the monster inside. Or if I did, I was too busy and or too self-absorbed to understand what I was seeing."

"That's called a lack of interest, Isabella."

"I know. I just…" She stared into the fog at her feet. "I'm not sure what I think, actually, what I missed, what I could have prevented if I'd been more aware. He called me all kinds of names, made references to situations that didn't apply to anything we'd been through or done. I realized then that he was mixing Aaron and Sybil up with us, inserting their story into ours. Not that we had a particular story, but you get the idea. His mind was gone, probably had been for years. And I didn't see it."

"Neither did his legal partner, or his clients, or your cousin."

"Katie never liked him."

"Not liking someone is a far cry from suggesting that person's insane."

"You're trying to make me feel better, aren't you?"

With a smile quirking his lips, he started toward her. "No more than you're trying to shift the subject from one Dark descendant to another. You dated Gimbel for two months, yet in all that time you never guessed anything was wrong?"

This time she spotted the trap. "Guessed it, no, but I didn't want to be with him, so even if I didn't understand why, I knew enough to back off. We may not always rely on them, but as a species, we do possess certain instincts."

"We also possess certain propensities."

A smile blossomed as he came back into touching range. "Yours is to believe the worst about yourself." She ran a suggestive finger over his chest. "Mine is to take risks. So who wins the battle of wills?"

"Maybe neither of us."

"Or maybe both? You're nothing like David, Donovan. For all her bad judgment, neither is Darlene. George is a sweetheart, Haden's a teddy bear—and you're going to kiss me again, aren't you?"

"Thinking about it."

He splayed his hands on her waist, held her gaze with his. "This could be a very big mistake."

"Risk taker," she reminded. Eyes dancing, she shifted her hips against him, slid her arms around his neck. "Now, about that kiss—"

His mouth covered hers before she finished the word. Heat and hunger and need fired up fast, sucking every errant thought from her head. An entirely different set of instincts surged to life. She thought the fog might actually be sparkling when Donovan trailed his lips along her jaw to her neck.

She tipped her head sideways, marveled at the delicious

buzz in her brain. "If Aaron had kissed Sybil like that, she'd never have left him."

"Wouldn't have made him any more sane."

"I'm not sure she'd have cared."

Once again his dark eyes fixed on hers. "I love you, Isabella, but you're playing with hellfire here."

"Love you, too, Black, and having been to hell and back recently, I'll go for the burn."

"Gimbel's…"

"Dead. Darkwood Manor's mine, and even if the ghosts we saw and heard weren't the real deal, the story will draw tourists to Mystic Harbor in droves. What's hellish about that?"

"You decide." Turning her to face the hazy outline of the manor, he dipped his head so his mouth brushed her ear. "I talked to Darlene, Isabella. She wrote that note warning you to leave town, and she was responsible for all the unearthly wails, but she swears on her grandfather's grave, the voice you heard at the manor telling you to run and not come back wasn't hers."

Harlequin INTRIGUE

COMING NEXT MONTH

Available March 8, 2011

#1263 RANSOM FOR A PRINCE
Cowboys Royale
Lisa Childs

#1264 AK-COWBOY
Sons of Troy Ledger
Joanna Wayne

#1265 THE SECRET OF CYPRIERE BAYOU
Shivers
Jana DeLeon

#1266 PROTECTING PLAIN JANE
The Precinct: SWAT
Julie Miller

#1267 NAVY SEAL SECURITY
Brothers in Arms
Carol Ericson

#1268 CIRCUMSTANTIAL MARRIAGE
Thriller
Kerry Connor

HICNM0211

REQUEST YOUR FREE BOOKS!
2 FREE NOVELS PLUS 2 FREE GIFTS!

Harlequin

INTRIGUE

BREATHTAKING ROMANTIC SUSPENSE

YES! Please send me 2 FREE Harlequin Intrigue® novels and my 2 FREE gifts (gifts are worth about $10). After receiving them, if I don't wish to receive any more books, I can return the shipping statement marked "cancel." If I don't cancel, I will receive 6 brand-new novels every month and be billed just $4.24 per book in the U.S. or $4.99 per book in Canada. That's a saving of at least 15% off the cover price! It's quite a bargain! Shipping and handling is just 50¢ per book in the U.S. and 75¢ per book in Canada.* I understand that accepting the 2 free books and gifts places me under no obligation to buy anything. I can always return a shipment and cancel at any time. Even if I never buy another book, the two free books and gifts are mine to keep forever.

182/382 HDN FC5H

Name _____ (PLEASE PRINT)

Address _____ Apt. #

City _____ State/Prov. _____ Zip/Postal Code

Signature (if under 18, a parent or guardian must sign)

Mail to the Reader Service:
IN U.S.A.: P.O. Box 1867, Buffalo, NY 14240-1867
IN CANADA: P.O. Box 609, Fort Erie, Ontario L2A 5X3

Not valid for current subscribers to Harlequin Intrigue books.

**Are you a subscriber to Harlequin Intrigue books
and want to receive the larger-print edition?
Call 1-800-873-8635 or visit www.ReaderService.com.**

* Terms and prices subject to change without notice. Prices do not include applicable taxes. Sales tax applicable in N.Y. Canadian residents will be charged applicable taxes. Offer not valid in Quebec. This offer is limited to one order per household. All orders subject to credit approval. Credit or debit balances in a customer's account(s) may be offset by any other outstanding balance owed by or to the customer. Please allow 4 to 6 weeks for delivery. Offer available while quantities last.

Your Privacy—The Reader Service is committed to protecting your privacy. Our Privacy Policy is available online at www.ReaderService.com or upon request from the Reader Service.

We make a portion of our mailing list available to reputable third parties that offer products we believe may interest you. If you prefer that we not exchange your name with third parties, or if you wish to clarify or modify your communication preferences, please visit us at www.ReaderService.com/consumerschoice or write to us at Reader Service Preference Service, P.O. Box 9062, Buffalo, NY 14269. Include your complete name and address.

HI11

USA TODAY *bestselling author Lynne Graham*
is back with a thrilling new trilogy
SECRETLY PREGNANT, CONVENIENTLY WED

Three heroines must marry alpha males to keep
their dreams…but Alejandro, Angelo and Cesario
are not about to be tamed!

Book 1—JEMIMA'S SECRET
Available March 2011 from Harlequin Presents®.

JEMIMA yanked open a drawer in the sideboard to find Alfie's birth certificate. Her son was her husband's child. It was a question of telling the truth whether she liked it or not. She extended the certificate to Alejandro.

"This has to be nonsense," Alejandro asserted.

"Well, if you can find some other way of explaining how I managed to give birth by that date and Alfie not be yours, I'd like to hear it," Jemima challenged.

Alejandro glanced up, golden eyes bright as blades and as dangerous. "All this proves is that you must still have been pregnant when you walked out on our marriage. It does not automatically follow that the child is mine."

"'I know it doesn't suit you to hear this news now and I really didn't want to tell you. But I can't lie to you about it. Someday Alfie may want to look you up and get acquainted."

"If what you have just told me is the truth, if that little boy does prove to be mine, it was vindictive and extremely selfish of you to leave me in ignorance!"

Jemima paled. "When I left you, I had no idea that I was still pregnant."

"Two years is a long period of time, yet you made no attempt to inform me that I might be a father. I will want DNA tests to confirm your claim before I make any decision about what I want to do."

"Do as you like," she told him curtly. "*I* know who Alfie's father is and there has never been any doubt of his identity."

"I will make arrangements for the tests to be carried out and I will see you again when the result is available," Alejandro drawled with lashings of dark Spanish masculine reserve.

"I'll contact a solicitor and start the divorce," Jemima proffered in turn.

Alejandro's eyes narrowed in a piercing scrutiny that made her uncomfortable. "It would be foolish to do anything before we have that DNA result."

"I disagree," Jemima flashed back. "I should have applied for a divorce the minute I left you!"

Alejandro quirked an ebony brow. "And why didn't you?"

Jemima dealt him a fulminating glance but said nothing, merely moving past him to open her front door in a blunt invitation for him to leave.

"I'll be in touch," he delivered on the doorstep.

What is Alejandro's next move? Perhaps rekindling their marriage is the only solution! But will Jemima agree?

Find out in Lynne Graham's
exciting new romance
JEMIMA'S SECRET

Available March 2011
from Harlequin Presents®.

Start your Best Body today with these top 3 nutrition tips!

1. SHOP THE PERIMETER OF THE GROCERY STORE: The good stuff—fruits, veggies, lean proteins and dairy—always line the outer edges of the store. When you veer into the center aisles, you enter the temptation zone, where the unhealthy foods live.

2. WATCH PORTION SIZES: Most portion sizes in restaurants are nearly twice the size of a true serving and at home, it's easy to "clean your plate." Use these easy serving guidelines:
- Protein: the palm of your hand
- Grains or Fruit: a cup of your hand
- Veggies: the palm of two open hands

3. USE THE RAINBOW RULE FOR PRODUCE: Your produce drawers should be filled with every color of fruits and vegetables. The greater the variety, the more vitamins and other nutrients you add to your diet.

Find these and many more helpful tips in

YOUR BEST BODY NOW
by
TOSCA RENO
WITH STACY BAKER

Bestselling Author of
THE EAT-CLEAN DIET

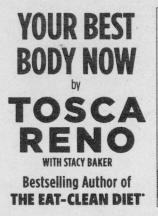

Available wherever books are sold!